YOU BET YOUR LIFE

YOU BET YOUR LIFE

Stuart M. Kaminsky

St. Martin's Press · New York

Library of Congress Cataloging in Publication Data

Kaminsky, Stuart M
  You bet your life.

                  I. Title.
PZ4.K1497Yo   [PS3561.A43]   813'.5'4   78-4016
ISBN 0-312-89662-X

To The Gordons:
Ida, Sylvia, Leonard, Tom, Sue and Jennifer

"Madman! Rising between us is a flowing river of blood.
How can I call him brother who tore away my hopes?"

Act III, Scene 8
La Forza D'el Destino
by Francesco Maria Piave

The narrow white pier pointed into Biscayne Bay like the finger of a rotting skeleton. The paint was peeling and the planks were soft under my feet from too many years of relentless salt water. A fat man sat or squatted at the far end of the pier—I couldn't tell if there was a chair under him, because he was wearing a long white terrycloth robe that made him look like a soggy tennis ball. His back was to me as I approached, but I could see a thin fishing pole in his oversized fingers. He didn't move. Dark clouds chased each other in the afternoon sky and the rickety pier danced with the white-topped waves. After a minute or two of watching him slowly being eroded by the Atlantic Ocean, I cleared my throat.

The fat man had to turn completely around to see me since there was no longer a clear separation between his head and neck, if one had ever existed. His face was a blank brown circle marred by a distinct dark scar that ran from below his left ear across his cheek. His eyes were as black as the sea behind him. An unlit cigar drooped in the corner of his thick mouth. He was almost bald, but a few strands of hair on top stood upright, comically blown by the warm wet wind.

"Mr. Capone," I shouted over the surf. "My name is Toby Peters."

The clouds had created a thick filter in front of the sun, but Al Capone cupped the chunky fingers of his left hand to shade an unnecessary squint as he examined me silently.

I turned back to the point where the pier touched the land and looked at the man who had led me there. His name was Leonardo, and I though he might give me some idea of how to handle things. But he simply stood with his arms folded, listening.

"I'm a private investigator, Mr. Capone—"

Capone interrupted with a sound that reminded me of someone chewing sand.

"I didn't catch that," I said, wiping water from my brow and tasting sea salt on my tongue.

Capone's answer was to turn away and fish again. I stood quietly for another minute or so while the waves and Florida humidity turned my light brown suit to moist black. A fish or mermaid tugged at Capone's line; then it was gone. Capone reacted much too late by jerking the pole out of the waves. There was no longer any bait on the hook. He hit the water three or four times with the pole, hoping to split the skull of the unprepared fish.

"Bastard," he mumbled, and began to fish again without bait.

It was 1941—February 19, 1941—and I was forty-four years old. The world was moving fast, a war was coming, and I was a private eye with one wet suit and fifty-six dollars in the bank. I imagined myself standing forever on this pier watching Al Capone fishing baitless while the salt of the sea calmly seeped through my undershirt. I almost fell asleep imagining it.

"Well?" said Capone, without turning around.

"A guy I knew said you might help me," I said. Capone watched the water. "The guy's name was Marty Maloney—Red Maloney. He was on the Rock with you."

Capone said nothing. I thought he grunted, so I went on.

"I'm working for MGM, the movie studio, on something you might be able to help with. Chico Marx is in some gambling trouble, and—"

"I remember Red," said Capone. "I don't forget my friends. We used to look out at night at the water and see Oakland and the fishing boats, and I told Red when I got out I'd sit and fish outside and no one would tell me to stop."

Capone looked up at the sky and watched two clouds separate to let the sun through for a second or two.

"I was in prisons for—I don't know—six years. They tried to rub me out on the Rock—hit me with a pipe. One time a Texas punk got me with a scissors in the back. I almost broke an arm pulling it out. Red and some other friends took care of the punk when they let him out of the dark. You said you know Red."

This time he turned to look at me, and then past me as if some inspiration might come. We both listened to the waves for a beat. Capone's eyes leaped suspiciously from Leonardo, fifteen yards away with his arms folded, to the asphalt road forty yards further where a Dade County police car was parked. A man in uniform was leaning against the door.

"You a cop?" Capone said, looking at the cop.

"No," I said. "I'm a private investigator. I don't get along with cops."

"Right," said Capone looking back at me. "Shoot. Tell your story."

I loosened my tie, which was slowly strangling me as it picked up seawater, and squatted down to take some pressure off my aching back and be at eye level with Capone.

"Chico Marx is one of the Marx Brothers," I said, not sure whether he would snarl at me for stating the obvious or take in the information as an important item.

"The Italian one," said Capone softly, with a knowing movement of the head. "That don't cut nothing special with me. I ain't Italian. I was born right here in this country in Brooklyn."

"Right," I said. Something wasn't right with Big Al. I remembered reading in the papers that about three years earlier, when Capone was getting ready to come out of jail, Jake Guzik had visited him in prison and told the press that Big Al was "nuttier than a fruitcake." The papers had said Al wasn't the first to go stir crazy on Alcatraz. I didn't know that guys stayed stir crazy two years after they got out, but *this* Al Capone was clearly not the man who had ruled a city with a buck and a chopper. I decided to plunge into my tale, get it told fast, and get the hell out of there and into dry clothes.

"Couple of weeks ao," I began talking fast, "Chico Marx was working in Vegas, leading a band. He got a call from Chicago. Guy identified himself as Gino. No last name. Acted as if Marx should know him. This Gino said Marx owed him 120 grand he lost on bets in Chicago and Cicero at Christmas. Marx thought it was a gag and hung up. He hadn't been in Chicago at Christmas. He was busy enough losing his money in Las Vegas without side trips. Gino called back, said it was no joke and Marx better come up with the money. Couple of days later Marx got a box in the mail with somebody's ear in it and a not very funny note telling him to hurry and pay or his brothers would get his piano fingers in a box."

"Brothers?" said Capone.

"The Marx Brothers."

"Yeah," said Capone. "I had them out to the club in Cicero once." Capone looked in the general direction of Cicero. "I had all the big ones—the Jew singers and comics. Cantor, Jessel, Sophie Tucker, the Ritz Brothers. I didn't know what was supposed to be funny about the Ritz brothers, but I gave them real nice watches. Cantor made some joke about dancing in concrete shoes, but I gave him a watch too. I gave a lot of people things they don't remember."

I nodded my head and went on with my tale. "Well,

Chico Marx has done a lot of gambling and a lot of losing, but he says this is a bum rap. Even if it wasn't a bum rap he doesn't have $120,000 right now. He doesn't want to be mailed to his brothers whole or in pieces, but he's not going to try to borrow money for something he doesn't owe. I want to find this Gino and ask why he's trying to get Marx. There must be some mistake. Can you help me?"

I'd left out a lot, like Louis B. Mayer's desire to keep the Marx Brothers from bad publicity. Mayer didn't like the Marx Brothers. He thought they were about as funny as Capone found Eddie Cantor and the Ritz Brothers. But *Go West* was out and doing well, and the Marxes owed Metro one more picture. Mayer wanted to start shooting with three brothers, not two. He didn't think there'd be much box office potential in Marx Brothers movies if Chico met a knife or bullet.

Capone's head was nodding in understanding.

"I'm a good citizen," he finally said, pulling his eyes away from the direction of the Mecca of Cicero. "You check with Colonel McCormick back in Chicago, at the *Tribune*. I stepped in and settled that newsboys strike when no one could handle it. Without me there wouldn't have been any news for days, maybe weeks. I even helped the Feds with stuff."

"And?" I prodded.

"I don't know no Gino," said Capone. "I mean, I know lots of Ginos but I've been away from it too long. I didn't see any friends on the Rock. No letters. I lost touch. It went by." His fat left hand went up in the air to show things going by, and then rested on the deep scar on his left cheek. His middle finger traced the rut of the scar as he chewed on his cigar.

He coughed or sighed, removed the cigar, and spat in the water.

"Pace, pace, mio Dio," said Capone softly. "Cruda sventura m'astringe, ahime, a languir. Come il di primo da taut' anni dura profondo il mio soffrir." Capone looked up at me. "That's Italian."

"I figured," I said.

"It's Verdi, *La Forza D'el Destino*," he explained. "It means 'Peace, peace, gimme peace God. Because of bad luck I have to sit around doing nothing. My grief is great.' Beautiful, huh?"

"It's beautiful," I said.

Capone spat another piece of his cigar into the Atlantic.

"Go to Chicago," he grunted. "Find my brother Ralph, or Nitti or Guzik or the mayor. He owes me. I got him elected. Tell them I said you were O.K. They can call me and check. They'll find this Gino."

"Thanks," I said, getting up and wondering what, if anything, I could do with the information.

"If you see Red," Capone said dropping his voice, "tell him Snorky said hello. You got that?"

"Snorky said hello. I got it."

"Good," added Capone, pointing a fat finger at me. "Good. You know I learned to play banjo on the Rock? Red remembers. I wrote a song for my mother."

His fat body under the robe tightened suddenly and shuddered. I think it was rage, but I couldn't tell for sure because he turned his head away. He threw the fishing pole into the water and looked across the waves. The interview was clearly over.

I had something I might be able to use—the name of Al Capone—though I didn't know what it was worth. I was also wet. My plan was find a hotel, change clothes, and decide what to do next.

I wobbled off the swaying pier and stood next to Leonardo. He looked like an inverted pyramid—his legs were thin and his upper body broad. He probably couldn't run worth a damn, but if he caught whatever he was chasing, his arms and shoulders could melt it like a sugar cube in hot water. If he couldn't catch what he was chasing, the gun bulging under his jacket could make up for a lot of distance. His dark face showed no teeth. He barely opened his mouth when he spoke. A neat round patch of hair on top of his head was white and unnatural, as if a finger of fire had scorched him. I wondered why, but had no intention of asking.

"You heard him?" I asked, glancing at the house to our left as we walked toward the waiting police car. The house was big, white, and made of wood. It was no mansion. We walked past a swimming pool with a life preserver bobbing in the middle.

"Al's brother Ralph paid off this place when Al was in the can," Leonardo volunteered. "Fifty grand. I don't think Big Al has a dime of his own."

I repeated my question: "You heard what we said out there?"

Leonardo grunted as we walked, then he spoke softly. We were far enough from the shore so the sound of the waves didn't come between us.

"My job's to hear. To be sure Al don't say anything that might not be good for whoever hears it."

We were a few dozen yards from the road.

Leonardo whacked a palm tree with his open hand. I assumed it was his way of communing with nature and expressing his joy of life. I never communed with nature. It got me nowhere and gave me a backache. Leonardo kept walking. I sloshed.

"And if Al had said something embarrassing?"

"Some I warn. You wouldn't take a warning."

I'm five-nine and 165 pounds dripping wet, which I was at that moment. My face was benign when I was twelve, but it had gradually become semimalignant. My nose was almost flat from too many encounters with an older brother who was now a cop, and my business scars ran, and still run, from my big toe to my forehead. Leonardo thought I looked tough. I'm reconstituted scar tissue and bone, tentatively glued together by a kid doctor in L.A. named Parry. Leonardo could have given me the chance to take a warning. But he was right. I probably wouldn't have taken it.

I looked straight ahead as we reached the road.

"You know the guy I was talking about, this Gino?" I said, drawing back my upper lip.

"Naw," said Leonardo, eyeing the waiting cop. The cop eyed him back from behind dark blue sunglasses.

"I've been here about a year. Like Al, I'm a little out of touch."

Leonado shrugged and headed back toward the pier. I took a last look at "Snorky" Capone. He was sitting like a melting snowman with his body turned seaward. I crossed the road and got into the cop car.

The cop got in and adjusted his tan sheriff's hat with the strap behind his head like Black Jack Pershing. He didn't know that I knew he was almost bald. I had spotted him removing his hat while I walked with Leonardo. It gave me secret, useless information to compensate for the fact that there wasn't a wrinkle or the sign of a wrinkle in his tight brown uniform. If he took off his mirror-shined brown shoes, his socks would be tailor made and odorless. The car was as neat as he was. I was sure he hated firing his pistol because it made the barrel dirty. His smile was fixed, but whatever he was smiling about was his alone, and he didn't plan to share it.

"Simmons," I said, as he pulled away. I had cleverly deduced his name from the silver plate over his left shirt pocket. "Simmons, that man is stir crazy. You could have—"

"No he's not," said Simmons, gunning his Dodge past a truck full of watermelons and down a highway lined with heavy, tired green trees sagging under huge leaves. Louis Garner Simmons had the kind of down-home drawl I never could get used to.

"Capone's got the tods, gator fever, Cuban itch, symph, venereal disease, whatever you want to call it. His brain is getting eaten up."

Simmons had not taken me to see Capone by choice. The order had come from a captain who got his order from a local political boss who got a call from a Miami lawyer who did some work for MGM. That put Simmons far down the line, and made him angry. He was probably as clean in thought, word, and deed as he was in uniform, and the idea of being an escort for someone who wanted to talk to Capone pleased him not at all.

Simmons shot a glance at me without turning his

head. What he saw didn't please him—a wilted California lump making a puddle on his vacuumed seat. I was a contaminant he wanted to get rid of. He gunned the engine and we shot forward, hitting sixty-five.

"Capone got syphilis years ago," he said. "It's in his records. He knew it probably, but he was scared of the needle for the test. That's a God's fact. You beat that? Son of a bitch shot men down, got shot and cut himself, but he's turning to jelly 'cause he was afraid of a needle. They finally tested him on the Rock after he blacked out one morning. But it was too late to do much. Some New York doctor comes down here every month giving him a new medicine, pencil-in, but that fat taxpayer's a dying man."

The idea of Capone dying tickled Simmons so much that he barely missed an old lady going fifteen miles an hour in an antique Ford. We were on a narrow strip of land with the Atlantic Ocean on our left and Biscayne Bay on our right.

"Why the rush?" I said, bracing myself with one hand on the windshield and one on the door handle.

"Got to get you to the train," he said, reaching over to remove my hand from the window and wiping my hand print off with a cloth drawn from his pocket. Even the cloth was unwrinkled. "You can catch the *City of Miami* at 5:25 and be in Chicago by 9:55 tomorrow night."

My bag was in the back of his car. I hadn't even had time to check into a hotel after I got off the morning plane from Atlanta.

"I thought I might stick around here for a few days," I said.

He pursed his lips, shook his head no and said, "You wouldn't like it."

Before I could think of a comment, he turned on his car radio with the volume high. Instead of police calls, we got Artie Shaw playing "Frenesi." The rest of the ride was uneventful, if we don't count the kid on the bike we almost killed on Biscayne Boulevard and the two pregnant women who dodged out of our way as we screeched around a corner onto Second Street. Artie Shaw's clarinet seemed to match the action. I saw what looked like a train station coming, so I braced myself without touching the window.

Simmons reached back for my suitcase, lifted it effortlessly into the front seat, dropped it in my lap and reached past me to open the door when we stopped.

"Does this mean you don't want to be pen pals?" I said.

"Have a nice trip," he replied through a white-toothed grin. "Got a feeling people are going to be expecting you in Chicago." He pronounced it *She-cawh-goo*, with as much contempt and Vitamin C as he could squeeze into an orange juice drawl. I got out. He got out and followed, but not closely enough so I could reopen conversation. Inside the station, he leaned against a wall after checking it carefully for cleanliness. I bought my ticket.

The ticket man told me to hurry and I did, leaving foot-print puddles across the tile floor. The *City of Miami* had its steam up, and I cleared the iron step as the train jerked forward. Simmons was on the platform with his arms folded, making sure I didn't get off. I had spent less than six hours in the sun and fun capital of the world.

Instead of heading for a seat and making it too wet to sit in for the next twenty-four hours, I balanced my way to a rocking washroom. I hailed a porter, got a hanger, and changed into my only other pair of pants. The pants had a crease in the knees where they had been folded into the case over a wire hanger. The crease wouldn't come out.

I hung up my suit and opened the window to dry it as fast as possible. It might be a little stiff, but it would be wearable.

Outside the window I caught a glimpse of a station that said we were going through Hollywood. For a second I thought time had slipped me a Mickey, or I had taken one too many in the head. I decided instead that there were two Hollywoods. Florida's was a little burg we shot through in less than six seconds.

A guy with a pot belly, tweed suit, vest, and a grey-brown beard came into the washroom humming. He looked at me and decided not to hum and not to stay. I looked in the mirror to see what had scared him and I saw. My hair tumbled over my bloodshot eyes and my teeth were clenched.

I brushed my hair back with my hand, soaked my eyes in cold water, and persuaded my teeth to relax. The water began to slosh around the toilet as we picked up speed. By the time we flew through Fort Lauderdale ten minutes later, I had had enough. I left my suit hanging and headed for the dining car. A little red flower bounced in a glass holder on the table where I was led by a waiter. Two fat women with that Southern accent I so loved sat across from me, talking about Corine's children. I tried not to listen, but I discovered anyway that Corine's children were disrespectful and should have been given the stick by Andy. The rest of the diners heard it too. The fat woman who suggested the stick looked up at me. I nodded in agreement of corporal punishment for children as I took a big bite of tuna on white and looked out the window at a lake. An alligator slithered out of the water. I had never seen an alligator before. I had never found a piece of wood in a tuna sandwich before either, but I did now and spat it out while the fat women watched me in disgust. By West Palm Beach the two ladies were gouging chasms in their peach melba, and I was nibbling soggy potato chips and drinking beer while I looked for more gators in the sunset. I didn't see any. I should have been thinking about where I was going and what I was going to do when I got there.

By Fort Pierce my suit was dry and slightly stiff. I carried it on a hanger to my seat as the sun went down and the Florida East Coast Railway carried me through New Smyrna Beach. When Louis Garner Simmons ran me out of Miami, I had acted cheap and bought a coach seat without even asking about compartments, even though the freight was being paid by Louis B. Mayer. Habits are hard to break. My seat was next to one of the fat ladies from the dining car. She looked up at me over bifocals as we went through Daytona Beach, and then she turned back to the book on what remained of her lap.

I glanced over her shoulder at the book—no mean task considering the size of her shoulder.

"How'd you like an elbow in your neck?" she said, giving her subtle opinion of literary eavesdropping. Her voice rang clear enough to be heard back in Miami in spite of the noise of the train. Her eyes didn't leave the page. Then she turned her gaze on me. We had clearly begun a beautiful friendship—the start of a trainboard romance.

"No thanks," I said.

The book she was reading was *The Grapes of Wrath*. I hadn't read it, but I had seen the movie. I decided to cement our relationship.

"Tom Joad joins the Commies at the end," I whispered.

The fat lady threw her elbow back, hitting my shoulder and letting out a massive grunt. The conductor, who looked old enough and mean enough to have been John Wilkes Booth's accomplice, came running down the aisle. His lip was turned up on one side in a pained sneer, and his ticket punch was held high like a weapon.

"What's the trouble he-ah?" he said, making it clear that he and the woman were of the same tribe. I was outnumbered. If I struggled, four hooded Klansmen might thunder out of the baggage room and trample me.

Before anyone could answer, the lady hit me in the neck with a second book. A car full of people rose to stare and an infant began to howl. I could swear that it howled with a Cracker accent.

"Now listen, mister," sighed the conductor, "We don't want no trouble from your kind and no smart talk."

The lady tried to punch me with her chubby arms but I backed away.

"He's bothering me," she said. "Insulting me."

"That true?" said the conductor.

"No," I said, "but—"

"Come with me," he said, and hurried down the aisle. I grabbed my suitcase and picked up the book the woman had thrown at me. It was an Agatha Christie novel, *The Peril at End House*. I had read that one.

I picked up my suit and leaned toward the woman over the conductor's outstretched boney arm and his hand holding a ticket puncher.

"Sorry ma'm," I whispered with a smile, knowing my smile resembled a twisted grimace, "but the girl did it in this one. She set up the whole thing to make it look like she was the victim."

The book came back at me as I tripped up the aisle escorted by the conductor and dozens of eyes. I could hear the pages flutter open as Hercule Poirot hit a wall and came down on some soprano who sang, "Hey?"

Nobody tripped me as I tried to keep up with the old conductor. I had a lot to be proud of. A Southern cop had run me out of Miami, so I had gained my revenge against the South by doing battle with a rotund belle of the rails. Maybe if the South had enough fat women, and I had enough time to provoke them, I could eventually gain my confidence back and destroy the Union.

Two cars down the old conductor stopped and

pulled his blue cap firmly over his eyes to show he
meant business. His face was filled with lines of grand-
fatherly wrath.

"Don't know what you did or said, son, but she
deserved it and more. Been shushing up the kids and
making loud remarks 'bout people. Come on. I'll buy
you a beer and you can take the rest of the trip in those
two empty seats over there where you can spread out
some."

His accent had come out soft and warm in spite of
an aged rasp, and I decided that it could be a pleasant
sound.

He was as good as his skinny word, and with a
second beer in me I was almost asleep when we hit
Jacksonville. Most of the lights were out in the car. it
was about midnight. Out the window on the platform a
couple of people were getting on. One was a skinny kid
in an orange shirt who looked up at the windows. I
thought his eyes rested on me. They were the glazed
eyes of a drunk, a junk, a punk, or all three. I looked at
him because he had no baggage and then I forgot him.
The ten minute layover and the vibration of the train
put me to sleep.

I dreamt I was working for Al Capone. There was a
party, and my job was to watch the guests' valuables and
coats. They began piling coats and jewels on a bed in a
small room. More and more guests came. My ex-wife
Anne came with George Raft and acted as if she didn't
know me. So far it was pretty true to life. Then Koko the
Clown also came to the party. Koko was a frequent star
of my dream world. I was also sure we were in Cincinnati. I dream about Cincinnati a lot, though I've never

been there. I've got an elaborate map of Cincinnati in my head from dreams.

I remember thinking that my dream was getting stupid, but the dream didn't stop. Coats, fur, and cloth piled up. I was running out of room, and the mound of clothes was about to topple over and smother me. I panicked and reached for my gun to shoot at the pile, but Al Capone's voice found me. "Is this the way you work for your friend Snorky?" he grunted. I reached out my hand and asked him to pull me out before I drowned in other people's wealth. Instead he sent in the Marx Brothers, a plumber, a manicurist, and a couple of trays of food. I complained about my bad back, tried to think of good deeds. "Cuts no ice with me," said Capone. "I'm a dying man. But you can have my scars."

I told him I didn't want his scars, that I had plenty of my own. He laughed, and I woke up with a stiff neck as the train pulled into Birmingham, Alabama, at 8:08 A.M. My mouth was dry. My face felt like a well-used toothbrush, and seated next to me at the window was the thin young man with the orange shirt who had gotten on in Jacksonville without a suitcase. He had his chin in his hand and his face away from me so I couldn't see his eyes. All I could see was his washed out, thin yellow hair and a bristly neck. I said "Good morning." He said nothing. I tilted my seat back, closed my eyes and tried to think. I got nowhere, so I went to the washroom, shaved, brushed my teeth, and went to the dining car where I had two bowls of cereal—one *Quaker Rice* and the other *Wheaties*. When I got back to my seat, the young man hadn't moved. Someone had either covered him with quick-drying lacquer, he was an Indian Yogi, or he was dead. I didn't care which. By early evening my always unreliable back was bothering me from sitting too long, and I had worked out a brilliant plan—I would do what Capone had suggested. I would try to find Ralph Capone, Nitti, or Guzik. I'd use Al's name and hope they'd help.

Satisfied with my mental effort, and feeling friendly, I asked the young guy if he was going to dinner. He hadn't moved for lunch. He grunted something and didn't move. I went to the dining car and was enjoying a Salisbury steak and carrots until we pulled to a stop in Indianapolis and I looked out the window. The young blond guy in the orange shirt was standing on the platform, which was fine with me. What wasn't so fine was that he was holding my suitcase. I reached for my wallet to throw down a couple of dollars on the table but the wallet was gone. The waiter shouted "wait" but I didn't wait. The young guy hadn't seen me. He might still think I was sitting unsuspecting over a steak I couldn't pay for. I jumped off the train with the steam of the engine drifting back to give me some cover.

I could tell it was cold, but I wasn't paying attention. I was looking for someone. I spotted him walking fast down the platform. As I moved between people toward him I passed the dining car. The waiter was pounding on the window at me making enough noise so everyone on the platform looked, including the guy with my suitcase. He spotted me and broke into a run. He had at least twenty years and fifteen yards on me but he wasn't in good shape and he was carrying a suitcase with a few heavy items including a .38 automatic. Bad back or no bad back, I caught up with him in thirty yards when he ran into a woman carrying a two year old.

The woman fell but held onto the kid, and I jumped, hitting the young guy at the waist. I was on his back, hammering his face against the concrete. The woman with the kid sat screaming at us, but I only hit the thief's head once, and in spite of the blood I knew he had nothing worse than a broken nose. I turned him over, pulled my wallet from his jacket, and freed my suitcase from his hands.

I had some questions for him, and as I sat on his chest I knew he would answer. I wanted to know if I was a coincidence or someone had fingered me. And if so, who and why. But two things changed my mind. The *City of Miami* began to pull out, and about ten cars down on the platform a guy with a cop was hurrying toward us. I got up fast, carrying my bag and stuffing my wallet in my pocket. I stepped over the lady sitting on the ground. her kid smiled at me and I smiled back. The smile got him. He cried. I made the train with a jump that wrenched my back.

I leaned painfully out to watch the cop stop at the battered punk and help him up. I didn't think the thief would say much. He probably had a record, and he'd certainly have a lot of explaining if he tried to nail me. I fumbled for a pill in my suitcase and limped back to my seat in the dining car. There wasn't any water on the table. I took the flower out of the glass and used the water to wash down the pain pill. It tasted green.

"Trying to steal my suitcase," I explained to the waiter, pulling out a five and pushing it toward him. He pocketed the bill, asked if I was all right, and turned away.

I spent the rest of the trip in my seat minding my own business. We hit Chicago just at 10 p.m. The windows were frosted, and I could make out mounds of snow through the circle I rubbed clear with my sleeve. I put my suit jacket on even though it didn't match my pants. If no one invited me to a presidential inauguration, I would be all right. I thanked the old conductor and followed a Negro in a heavy coat down the metal steps and into a blast of cold Chicago air. It was night, but the train depot was bright with lights showing swept-up piles of dirty snow. It was the first time I had seen snow this close. I'd seen it on mountains, but never close enough to touch. I didn't stop to touch it. The cold cut me in half and kicked me in the back for good luck. Then it scratched at my teeth like a nail on glass. I pushed past people who were bundled to their eyes, prepared for the winter blast. Sprinting around a group of lunatic girls who were singing, I almost made it to a door that glowed warm, promising coffee. A hand grabbed my sleeve.

"Peters," said a deep voice, confident as doom.

The guy holding me was craggy faced and about fifty. His nose was red, but I couldn't tell if it was from the cold, alcohol, or both. He wore a coat and hat, but no scarf, and the coat wasn't buttoned tight. He seemed to ignore the cold. His grip was tight and mean, but on his face was a soft, tolerant smile, like he had seen everything and I was no surprise. Another hand grabbed my free arm, and I turned to see who was attached to it. It was a burly young cop in a dark blue coat and cap. He wasn't smiling. He looked unhappy, cold, and a little angry. I figured that the punk had tried to nail me in Indianapolis, and the call had come ahead.

"Yeah, I'm Peters," I said, "and I'm cold. Can we go inside?"

The fat lady with *The Grapes of Wrath* passed by us into the door. She saw the cop holding me and let out a triumphant trumpet, like a charging elephant I had once seen in a Tarzan movie. The elephant spewed out clouds of mist in the crisp cold air and disappeared forever.

The red nosed guy let go of my arm and nodded as if my request were reasonable. We pushed through the door and started up a concrete stairway.

"Welcome to Chicago," he said.

The waiting room of the station had a high-ceiling and was filled with wooden benches. It was a church with all the pews facing a big ad for Woodbury soap. There were a few people on the benches, but they weren't worshipping the soap for the skin you love to touch. Some were sleeping. Some were reading. Most were looking at each other, or nowhere.

The two cops led me slowly around the benches toward a short order counter that jutted out on one side of the hall and sent out a smell of sweet grease. There were lots of stools open. The plainclothes cop pointed to the one I should take. It had a piece of yellow food on it. He swept it away and waited for me to sit. The cops sat on either side of me. A semicatatonic woman sat next to the plainclothes cop, drinking yellow coffee and silently gnawing a sodden sweetroll.

I put my suitcase by my feet and watched a lemon-shaped waitress bring yellow coffee for the three of us without being asked. The cops were waiting for me to say something. I was waiting for them. I'd been a cop once and I'd stepped into mistakes often enough to know that you kept your mouth shut with cops until you had to talk.

"My name's Kleinhans," said the red-nosed guy, "Sergeant Kleinhans. You can call me Chuck or Kleinhans, whatever suits you. The gentleman on your right is Officer Jackson. You can call him Officer Jackson. Officer Jackson is about to take his coffee to that seat over there where he can be alone with his thoughts."

I shut up and drank my coffee from a thick, porcelin cup with a big handle. The coffee didn't taste bad. It had no taste. My cup was more interesting. It had a branching crack in it. I followed the crack with my eyes and let the steam of the coffee hit my face. Kleinhans gripped his cup in two hands.

"Hot cup against your palm on a cold night feels good," he said. I put on a wry grin and nodded my head knowingly. Kleinhans went on talking very softly into his cup without looking up at me.

"We got a call about you from Miami," he said. "Well, anyway, my boss got a call. Seems you're here to check up on something involving some of our good friends in the criminal world."

I was ready to say something, but having started, Kleinhans wanted to finish his piece.

"I work out of the Maxwell Street Station not too

far from here," he went on, savoring the feel of hot porcelin in his hands. "I sort of specialize in gambling problems related to the citizens in question. Would you like a roll?"

I said no, but that I would like some cereal. The waitress brought him a cheese Danish and me a bowl of what looked like Rice Krispies. Crumbs fell from Kleinhans' sugary Danish. He swept them off with the back of his arm. They snowed on the catatonic woman. She didn't complain.

"Maybe we can be of service to each other," Kleinhans went on. "I'll tell you how to get in touch with certain people, and you keep me informed about what you find out. Now this isn't exactly the way I'd play it with you if I had my way, but my boss says to treat you right. You've got connections. And who knows? You might come up with something I can use."

"You mean you might be able to use me?" I said.

He nodded his head sagely and said "mmm" as he wiped sugar from his mouth with a napkin.

"We understand each other," he beamed. "Here's my office number and home number." He pulled out a pencil and wrote two numbers on the napkin he had just used on his mouth. "Take it. Call me if and when, and at least once a day." He shrugged. "Trains and planes leave here every day for the bright sunshine of California. If I were you, Señor Peters, I'd get a ticket and head for the sun tonight. You're not dressed for our weather."

"I think I'll stick around."

"Figured you would," he said, clapping my back with a broad right hand. "No trouble from you—" he pointed to me, "no trouble from me," he pointed at himself. His pronoun references were unmistakable, but I wasn't exactly sure of what his definition of trouble might be.

"It's a deal," I said.

"Nope. It's the way I say things are going to be. We're not partners, Mike Shayne. Now, we'll drop you at a hotel where you can get some sleep, and you can give me call in the morning. You want to stay fancy or cheap?"

"It's on MGM," I said, "but I'm used to small rooms. Too much space makes me nervous."

"We'll compromise on the LaSalle." He got up, threw some money on the counter, glanced at Officer Jackson, and turned away. Jackson wasn't finished, but swallowed the rest of his donut and spilled some of his coffee on his uniform trying to get his money's worth.

The unmarked cop car was right outside the door in a no-parking zone. Kleinhans and Jackson walked to it slowly. It was no more than a few feet, but pain shot through my head.

"How cold is it?" I asked, getting into the front seat as directed. Jackson drove. Kleinhans sat in back. I wasn't a suspect, but one never knew.

"Eleven or twelve above," said Jackson. "Not too bad."

Kleinhans serenaded us with a whistled version of "San Antonio Rose." He even *buh-buh-buhed* like Bing Crosby a few times. No one talked until Jackson pulled over five minutes later and stopped in front of the LaSalle Hotel.

I said thanks and got out for my dash to the lobby,

but Kleinhans called for me to lean over.

"If the bad guys don't already know you're here, they will soon. May even have been somebody at the station watching for you. I didn't spot anybody, but we're probably not the only ones who got a call about you from Florida."

Officer Jackson looked out the opposite window. I was no fun anymore.

"I got you," I said. "Goodnight."

"Comparatively," said Kleinhans rolling up his window. I waited for the car to pull away. It didn't. So I went up the stairs into the lobby. The doorman tried to take my case, but I wasn't letting it out of my hands again.

It was eleven at night. There were lots of people in the lobby to watch me make my way to the desk in a stiff summer jacket and unmatched pants with a conspicuous crease at the knee. The suitcase didn't help. It was a second-hand piece I got for three bucks from a pawnshop owner in L.A. named Gittleson. I had muscled a teenage Mexican kid for him when the kid tried to buy a gun and wouldn't take no for an answer. I was a real class item for the LaSalle Hotel, yes I was.

The clerk on the desk gave me the electric smile with the eyebrows raised to ask what a creature like me wanted in a place like this. He looked like an unprissy version of Franklin Pangborn.

"I'd like a room," I said, reaching for the desk pen and dipping it in the inkwell. I dripped ink on the blotter while I waited for him to produce the guest book.

"What kind of room?" he said.

"One with a bed and a bath," I answered. "That's

what hotels usually have. It doesn't have to be big, just warm."

He tried to keep from nibbling his upper lip. I didn't look enough like a bum or a nut to be thrown out, but I didn't look quite respectable enough to stay. It was my running problem regardless of what clothes I wore, but it was more acute at the moment. People in the lobby were looking toward us, and both of us kept our voices down.

"I'll pay two days in advance," I said. "My name is Peters, Toby Peters of MGM."

The clerk's eyes opened in understanding and his head rose from despair.

"You're a movie person?"

"Yes," I said. "From Hollywood. I was there this morning."

The clerk obviously believed movie people were exempt from decent dress. He turned the guest book toward me. I signed.

"Yes, Mr. Peters," he beamed, "I've seen some of your work."

"Good," I said taking the key to 605 and shooing away the bellboy. I wondered which piece of work he had seen—the guy who fell out of my window in Los Angeles the year before when he tried to kill me, or maybe the flea bag desk clerk I had pushed around a few months ago.

A middle-aged couple got on the elevator with me. By middle age I mean they were a year or two older than me. The lower range of middle age went up miraculously each year, managing to stay just ahead of me. If I lived long enough, I might entirely eliminate middle age from my experience. Someday I'll just wake up and admit that I'm old.

The thought depressed me almost as much as I depressed the couple on the elevator. I didn't depress the elevator man. He just looked at his numbers and minded his own business. Up to now he was my favorite person in Chicago.

The couple got off at four. Before the door was closed, they whispered, "Who do you think—"

I got off at six, found the right door, and went in. My room was dark, carpeted, and small. I turned on the radio. Kate Smith was in the middle of "The Last Time I Saw Paris." I checked my gun and my cash. They were both there. I couldn't see anything out the window. It was frosted over. Light was coming through from LaSalle Street.

I went back in the hall and pushed the elevator button. It came up empty, and I offered the kid a quarter for the newspaper under his chair. He said I could get my own for two cents by riding down to the lobby. I didn't want to face the lobby again.

"I'm in the movies," I explained.

He understood, which was more than I did, and exchanged the paper for a quarter. I locked my door just as Kate sang "and every time I think of him, I'll think of him that way." I turned off the radio, ran a hot bath, took off my clothes and soaked my weary back while I read The Chicago Tribune, which told me it was "The World's Greatest Newspaper."

The headline said "30 Senators For War." Senator Burton K. Wheeler warned me about "war madness" and said Roosevelt was preaching "hate and fear." That cheered me almost as much as thinking about middle age, so I moved to another page where I found that the Nazis had attacked sixteen British merchant ships and destroyed twelve. At a mayors' conference, LaGuardia of New York told mayors to prepare for bombing attacks. Jews in Holland were being barred by the Nazis as blood donors. General Marshall was worried about Japan building up air power in the Pacific. He was answering by sending 500 troops to Manila. The Japs didn't worry me. I had the word straight from the dentist who shares my office in Los Angeles. Dr. Shelly Minck, who had voted for Wilkie, assured me that we could beat the Japanese in two weeks. That was reassuring, but I wondered what those 500 troops were going to do against airplanes.

Even Dick Tracy was depressing. Some guy in a small-town lockup was offering a constable a hundred bucks. "I'd like to take a trip to, say, California," said the balloon over the guy's head. So would I, I thought, and found some ads for stores selling coats so I could get a line on costs.

I took a pain pill for my back and went to bed. I dreamt about Cincinnati.

When I got up it was morning. At least my watch said it was morning. Outside the window it was as dark as the night before. A call to the desk said my watch was right and the sun would be rising in a few minutes. The desk added that we would probably never know when it came because of the cloud cover.

I brushed my teeth and shaved slowly with a new blade. Then I put on my last clean shirt and tie, and matched my jacket to my pants. I had an important job this morning—the purchase of a coat. I sneezed, blew my nose, and tried to hold back the possibility that I might be catching a cold. In Chicago you could die in days from a common cold. There were lots of other things you could die from in Chicago, but I hadn't faced them yet.

In the lobby I asked where the nearest clothing store was, and was told it was a block away. It was nine in the morning, and the temperature couldn't have topped nine or ten degrees over zero. It reminded me of a line from an old Bert Williams song—"Good Lord, I thought I was prepared, but I wasn't prepared for that."

The clothing store was warm, and I was in no mood to bargin. Their price was right—thirty bucks. I knew a little shopping could cut that in half, but I couldn't fight off pneumonia without a warm coat, and soon. Mayer owed me a coat. I'd sell it to Gittleson as soon as I got back to Los Angeles. The coat was warm and brown with big buttons. I threw in a hat, gloves, and ear muffs. The whole thing came to a little over forty bucks. I made a note of it in my traveling expense book.

Before heading back to my room, I stopped in a corner Steinway drug store for a couple of eggs, bacon, and toast. The place was jammed with people fortifying themselves for the day. A good looking woman next to me wore a suit with padded shoulders and a turban. I ordered some cereal and sneezed in her coffee. She had real class, and never acknowledged that I existed. After picking up a bottle of Bromo Quinine Cold Tablets, I headed back for the hotel to call Sergeant Kleinhans.

Maybe I shouldn't have bought the ear muffs. Maybe skipping breakfast or the cold tablets would have made the difference. The world is full of maybes and wishes. Some people live on them. I knew I hadn't been out of that hotel room more than forty minutes.

When I got back the door was the way I had left it, locked. I let myself in, went to the bathroom, had a handful of cold tablets, and went to find Kleinhans' number. I found it in my other pants. I was spreading the napkin out to read it when I noticed the closet door was open. I read about compulsions once in the Saturday Evening Post. My compulsions are as reasonable as the next guy's. Doors have to be closed, drawers have to be closed. Taps have to be turned off, and dishes can't be left overnight.

I kicked the closet door closed with my foot as I looked at the napkin, but the door didn't stay closed. It opened from the weight of the body behind it. He was a big man in a blue suit. He fell forward fast before I could see his face. All I saw was a splash of red across his chest. But identification was no problem. I could tell from the circle of white hair and the prone pyramid shape that Leonardo had made the trip from Miami to a closet in a Chicago hotel. I'd probably never know what caused that circle of white. My first reaction was to open my suitcase. My 38 was there, unfired. I called Kleinhans' number. He wasn't in. I left a message for him to call.

There wasn't much chance that Nitti, Capone or Guzik were listed in the phone book. A half hour earlier Leonardo could have told me. I went through Leonardo's pockets. Maybe I'd find something that would tell me what he was doing dead in my hotel room. His wallet had eighty dollars covered with blood and some family pictures—an old woman and three younger boys all of whom looked like Leonardo.

I called Louis B. Mayer, collect. He wasn't in. I left a message. I called the hotel in Las Vegas where Chico Marx was working. The switchboard operator said Mr. Marx couldn't be reached, and she sounded as if she had more to say but couldn't, or wouldn't. I left a message.

The phone rang, and Kleinhans was on the other end.

"You got a number or address for me?" I said calmly.

"I'll give you an address in a few hours. Just remember, keep in touch and let me know if you get anything."

"I've already got a couple of things," I said, looking down at Leonardo.

"You're fast," clucked Kleinhans. I could hear squad room noises behind him and tried to imagine the room. I expected to be in it within the hour.

"Well," I said, "I've got a cold."

"Sorry to hear it."

"I can take care of that," I said. "I bought a coat and some cold tablets. But I can't take care of the other thing, the guy with the bullet holes who just fell out of my closet."

After a pause, Kleinhans sent out a sigh I didn't need a telephone for.

"You're lucky you got me, Peters. Cops in Chicago don't like jokes about bodies."

"No joke," I said. "He's lying on my floor. According to his wallet, he's Leonardo Bistolfi. You know him?"

"I know him. Don't move. I'll be right there."

I had exhausted everything I could do to keep busy. I knew what would happen as soon as I put the phone down, and it did. The tremor started in my fingers. If I didn't do something, it would travel up my arms and into my legs. Then I'd start to sweat. If I didn't stop it then, the next step would be to give up my breakfast. I'd seen corpses before, too many of them, but there is something about finding one in your closet that kicks the crap out of professional distance. A smart-ass voice not too deep inside my chest tried to say, "It could have been you. It could have been you."

To drown out the voice and give my hands something to do, I sang Pinky Tomlin's "The Love Bug Will Get You If You Don't Watch Out," while I went through Bistolfi's pockets and clothes again.

By the time I sang "and when he gets you you will sing and shout", I had discovered that Leonardo Bistolfi bought his suit in Miami and had a thick ring of keys. A decorative metal disc on the key ring had the initials LVB on one side and the word "Fireside" in black enamel on the other. He had sixty-three cents in change, including an 1889 Indian head penny I was tempted to pocket for my nephew Dave who saved coins. I resisted temptation. It was easy. Besides a monogrammed white handkerchief in his jacket pocket and the wallet I'd already looked at, Bistolfi was empty.

I went through the wallet more carefully, but it told me nothing more. No membership cards. No notes. No numbers. No addresses, only Bistolfi's address in care of Capone, Palm Island, Miami, Florida. I had succeeded in stilling the voice inside me and moved on to my rendition of Tomlin's "What's The Reason I'm Not Pleasing You?" Then my eyes fell on Leonardo's bloody face. He was looking at me in surprise. I put the wallet back, washed my hands, and sat down to wait. My brain had stopped working. It needed a live human or two to get it running again.

Thirteen minutes later, Kleinhans and two uniformed cops were at the door. We all looked at the body for a while, with Kleinhans humming something I didn't recognize. He nodded to the older of the cops, who moved to the phone. People were gathering outside the open door, so the second cop, who he called Rourke, went outside and closed the door.

"You hear Rourke out there yelling?" said Kleinhans softly as he kneeled.

"No," I said. There was a hum of voices beyond the door.

"Rourke's a yeller. If we can't hear him, this room is the next best thing to soundproof. It'd have to be for someone to do this and not draw curious citizens like flies to Maxwell Street."

The fat cop was talking on the phone behind us, but he kept his voice down so I only caught a few words. It didn't take much to guess he was calling the Medical Examiner or Coroner or whatever they called it in Cook County.

"Chopper did that," said Kleinhans. "Relatively clean. Short burst. I'd say someone who knows how to handle it. No needless extra shots. The walls are clean."

"Maybe he was shot someplace else and brought here." I suggested, popping another Bromo tablet and blowing my nose into a wad of toilet paper.

Kleinhans sat down in the only chair in the room. I sat on the bed. The cop on the phone kept talking.

"Nope," said Kleinhans, pursing his lips and scratching his bulbous nose. "And you don't think so either. According to the stuff we got on you last night from L.A., you were a cop. Maybe not much of a cop, but a cop. How would anyone get a bloody corpse like that up to the sixth floor of a downtown Chicago hotel?"

"A better question is why." I said.

Kleinhans took his hat off, scratched his scalp like a nervous chimp and examined his fingernails to see what they had found. The cop hung up the phone and said, "They're on the way." Kleinhans rubbed his ear and nodded toward the door. The second cop left. I blew my nose.

"Better take care of that," he said.

"I'm trying," I said.

Kleinhans looked at the body for a few more seconds before speaking.

"Ever see our friend before?"

"Two days ago in Miami. He was keeping an eye on Capone for someone. Nitti, Guzik, or his brother Ralph. He didn't say."

"Must have come up by plane," he said. "You working some kind of deal with him?"

"Am I going to need a lawyer?"

"I don't think so," said Kleinhans, getting up. There was a knock at the door. He opened it and let the fat cop in. They talked without me for a few seconds.

"We've got to get out of here for awhile," Kleinhans said, putting a hand on my shoulder. "State Street district is a few minutes away. Let's ride down there and talk."

He was pretty good. He made it all sound like a friendly request. Doctor and patient. Dad and son. In Los Angeles I might have tested him, pulled back to see how mean he could get, but it wasn't in me. The cold in my head and outside the hotel were getting to me as much as Leonardo was.

"Right," I said. "Know why he had that circle of white hair on his head?"

"Beats me," said Kleinhans.

We were at the State Street Station in about five minutes and in an office Kleinhans borrowed from a lieutenant who was home with the flu. My brother's a cop with an office. My brother's office was small and almost as old as California. There was no room in it to run if Phil lost his temper, which was about eighty percent of the time. The Chicago lieutenant's office was a big cold barn with bare wooden floors and an echo. It looked as if someone years earlier had moved all the furniture into the middle of the room to get ready to paint the walls and then forgot about it.

"Tell your story," said Kleinhans, getting comfortable behind the desk with a cup of coffee. He gave me one, too. We both kept our coats on. I started my tale in Miami, worked my way forward to include my battle with the orange-shirted kid in the train, and made it up to Leonardo in the closet.

Kleinhans was looking out of the window at a passing streetcar when I finished.

"What do you think?" he said.

"I don't know. Someone went to a lot of trouble to dump the body on me. Maybe it's a warning. It might be a threat or a screwy accident. Maybe Leonardo decided I got something from Capone or I was on my way to something. Maybe he called Chicago for orders. Maybe he called the kid in Jacksonville and told him to grab my stuff so they could check me out. Maybe Leonardo decided to come here and stop me, but someone stopped him instead."

"And maybe elephants piss nickels," sighed Kleinhans, wrinkling his brow for a massive belch that never came.

"For what it's worth, I don't think you're lying," he said, finishing his coffee. "You don't have a chopper and you'd be one fool to kill a guy in your hotel room and call the cops. It smells like a gang job with you in the middle, but I don't see how or why. I've seen a lot of them put away like Leonardo. Thompson submachine gun bootlegged from a crooked Army supply sergeant somewhere or stolen by a mob kid who spent a few years in the army. Bullets are easy to get. Standard forty-five in ACP rimless cartridges, basic U.S. Army pistol round since 1900. The ammunition is held in a circular drum. Fifty rounds. Our expert at the LaSalle didn't need more than ten or twelve. He had a pro finger. Those things kick, but they're nice and easy to work. Just pull back the bolt, push the trigger, the bolt comes forward, throws a round into the magazine and pushes it into the chamber. The round pops into the chamber, drops in place. The firing pin on the bolt crushes the cap, and the bullet flies. The bolt kicks back from the shot, and another slug falls in the chamber. Two or three spit out every second. Takes a soft touch and strong hand to handle a chopper without making a mess."

"He was a mess," I said.

Kleinhans shook his head no.

"The St. Valentine's Day party was a mess. I was on the cleanup. I moved Frank Guzenberg. That was a mess. You want another coffee?"

"No," I said. "What are you going to do?"

"Have some coffee, Toby my friend. Were I you, I'd get the hell out of here. But I'm not you. I'm going to do nothing much except turn this over to some homicide boys. The hotel is in their district, and happy I am of it. Now I'm going to the can and getting some more coffee. Then you can go back to looking for your gangsters, but I've got a feeling one of them has already found you."

He left the room closing the door behind him. The phone on the desk gave me an idea. Kleinhans wasn't worried about the mob death of a bodyguard, but I had a lot of reasons for caring. One was that it must have had something to do with the Chico Marx business. The other was that death was too close to me. I blew my nose, took a deep breath and picked up the phone.

"Desk," came a tired voice.

"Get me Indianapolis Central Police Headquarters and move it fast. If you're too tired to move, we can get you out on the street."

The guy on the desk put the call through fast. He didn't want to be out on the streets of Chicago in the winter. I watched the door and waited. A voice came through the phone, a little tinny, but clear.

"Tashlin."

"This is Detective Peters in Chicago. You got a pencil?"

"Yeah."

"Write this number." I gave him the number on the phone. "Now check on a blotter report for last night. Kid in an orange shirt had his nose broken at the train station."

"Probably a local," Tashlin said through his teeth.

"Hey," I snarled. "You just find it. Don't guess. The mayor here wants it and he's on my ass. I don't know why he wants it or what's going on, but if he doesn't get it, I serve you on a platter, Tashlin. When our mayor gets mad, he knows how to use the phone and he's got your mayor's number. Got it?"

All he had to do was ask me who the mayor of Chicago was and the game was over, but he took the easy way out, which I figured he would. If he hadn't, nothing was lost.

"You want to call me back?" I said.

"No," he said. "Hang on."

I hung on and Kleinhans came back with his coffee. With my hand over the mouthpiece I explained.

"Local call. MGM office. I need some more cash and the name of a lawyer in case I need one."

"Next time you ask first."

"Sorry," I said. "I'll pay the nickel."

"Here's an address for you," said Kleinhans, pulling out his pencil and writing it on the torn end of a ratty blotter. You may find Nitti there or you can leave a message. There's no phone."

"Is it far?"

"You can almost walk it from here. It's over on twenty-second. We're on twelfth. Ten blocks almost straight."

"Thanks," I said.

"Your funeral, California," he grinned.

Tashlin came back on the line.

"Got it," he said anxious to please. "Kid named Canetta, Carl "Bitter" Canetta. Small time record in Chicago, Atlanta, Miami, Jacksonville. Said some guy tried to hype his suitcase. Ran off with it. A woman with a kid backed him up. You want her name?"

"No thanks," I said, smiling at Kleinhans. "You have an address for our friend, someplace I can reach him?"

"Canetta?"

"Right."

"Fourteen ten Ainslie in Chicago, but that's old. Said he was living at the Y in Indianapolis, but hadn't checked in yet."

"Thanks," I said. I hung up.

"Got what you want?" said Kleinhans.

"Not as much as I wanted," I said, looking at the address on the piece of blotter.

"Better stay away from your room for a few hours. I don't think they'll need to lock it up. There won't be any prints worth looking for. The homicide and coroner's crew give up easy on these, shove them under—grab the first guy handy or give it up. The papers don't even care much anymore."

"You can do something for me," I said.

"My goal in life," he answered.

"See if you have a recent address for a small timer named Carl Canetta."

"I'll check," he said, yawning.

I told him that was comforting, blew my nose, promised to call, and stepped out of the office. I wondered if that new medicine Leonardo had told me they were using on Capone was any good for a cold. I stopped in the toilet, stole a roll of paper for my nose, chewed my last Bromo tablet, and went out on State Street looking for a cab to take me to Frank Nitti.

The cab driver's name was Raymond Narducy, according to the name plate and picture. He was a little guy with glasses and a wooly blue scarf over most of his face. The heater in the cab wasn't working.

We headed south on the red bricks at State Street past dark-windowed bars and sprawling auto parts shops crushing two-story frame houses between them. In the window of one of the houses I spotted a little kid with her face pressed into, and distorted by, a cold glass pane.

"That's Colisimo's," Narducy said through his scarf. I looked. There was a sign saying *Colisimo's*. Without Narducy's warning I would have missed it. It was a three-floor brick building, nothing special.

"Big Jim Colisimo used to be the boss around

here," Narducy said. "Johnny Torrio gunned him and took over. Then he gave it all to Big Al. Big Al died in Alcatraz."

"That a fact?" I said. "Why you telling me? I look like a historian?"

"Naw," said Narducy, making a left turn on twenty-second Street. "You look like a cop. Wanna know how I knew you were a cop?"

"Yeah."

"One," he said, holding up a holey glove and extending a finger, "You came out of the police station. Now you could have been a criminal, but with that new coat and hat, if you were a criminal, you'd have a car. If you were a lawyer you'd have a car. If you were a bail bondsman, I'd know you. You look too tough to be a victim. You want more?"

"Sure," I said. He had pulled to a stop on the curb across from the place I was looking for, the New Michigan Hotel.

"Two," said Narducy, holding up a second finger, "You aren't a local cop. A local cop would have a car, too. Wouldn't take a cab. You're on an expense account of some kind. I saw you write something down in that little notebook. Three, you're from someplace warm—California. You're wearing a lightweight summer pants. Couldn't be Florida because you don't sound it. I know accents. For instance, you can always tell Canadians. They say *aboot* for about. I study human nature. Shit, I got nothing else to do except freeze and read detective stories. So," he said, holding up his whole hand, "I put all this together about you and with a few guesses, and the fact that you wanted to go to the New Michigan where I've delivered some unsavory ones, I come up with the following: You're a California cop tracking down some guy. You asked the Chicago cops for help and they didn't give you much so you're on your own."

"That gets you a quarter tip, Philo, and if you want to sit here with the meter off, I'll be back out in a little while."

"Suits me just plumb to death," he said in a fake Western accent. "You don't come out in an hour you want me to call the sheriff to send in a posse?"

"No," I said. "It'd be too late. By the way—Capone ain't dead. He's alive and not very well in Miami."

"I never claimed to be good on facts," said Narducy, looking at me in the mirror over his glasses. "It's deduction that's my forte."

"Goodbye," I said, turning to cross the street.

"Around here it's *arrivaderchi*," replied Narducy, wrapping his arms around himself and slouching for warmth.

The lobby of the hotel didn't look big time. Like the neighborhood, it had dropped from what had once apparently been near-respectability. It was almost noon. A couple of well-upholstered painted ladies sat on stuffed chairs. It was too early and too cold to go out and work. The hotel lobby had the musty smell of mildewed carpet. It was still a few years from being an out-and-out dive, but it was clearly a losing battle. As I walked to the desk, I spotted a mean looking guy shaped like an egg giving me the eye. He was sitting, but by the time I reached the desk he had put down his comic book and was heading toward me.

The dark young desk clerk sat with his chin in his hands and his elbows on the counter. He wore a suit, a tie, a cut on his chin from shaving, and the look of someone who had taken something to keep as much distance as possible between what he saw in his head and what his eyes told him was out there.

"I want to get a message to Frank Nitti," I whispered to the clark. The tough looking little fat guy listened. The clerk heard my voice from somewhere and looked in my general direction, trying to focus. He was probably the day talent. It didn't look like many people checked into the New Michigan during the day.

"What makes you think Mr. Nitti's here?" The fat little guy's voice was the croak of a frog through a tunnel of sandpaper.

I looked at the desk clerk who was just turning toward the gravel voice. I knew when I spoke he'd start to turn back to me and he'd forever be a beat behind whoever was talking. He must have felt like someone watching a movie out of synch. From the gentle grin, I gathered he liked it that way.

"A cop told me," I said, still looking at the desk clerk. The fat guy cut the distance between us to almost nothing and breathed garlic up at me. He must have been eating the stuff for breakfast.
"I've got a message for Nitti from Big Al," I said, fascinated by the desk clerk's underwater movement. "I got in from Miami last night."

"Who are you?" he croaked.

"My name's Peters, Toby Peters. Big Al said Nitti would help me with something. Said he was a good guy."

From the corner of my eye I could see the fat face nod in agreement about Nitti being a good guy. From what I knew about Nitti, he had been Capone's enforcer, the top killer. With Capone gone, he might be on top instead of Ralph Capone or Guzik. I didn't know. I thought I'd ask Kleinhans the next time I saw him.

"Wait here," said the fat man. He walked away and around a corner.

"Large weather we're having," I said to the desk clerk, who nodded in agreement.

The ladies of the afternoon looked me over, gave me their best show of teeth, ankle, thigh and breast. I shrugged sadly, pointed upstairs and said, "Business." They went back to their conversation.

I blew my nose two or three times, passed my hand in front of the clerk's face to be sure he wasn't blind, and waited. The fat guy came back in about five minutes and waved a ham hand at me to follow. I followed. We got on an elevator just big enough for the fat guy and me, or four normal people. I listened to him breathe hard over the clank of the box we were in. There wasn't enough room to blow my nose.

We got out on five and went down a very narrow corridor. I knew which room we were going to. A guy in a dark suit who looked like Lon Chaney in one of his better disguises stood in front of a door with his arms folded. He gave me a sneer, opened the door behind him, and stepped in. The fat guy stood behind me.

The room smelled like fried chicken left overnight. It probably was fried chicken. The new Michigan was full of nostalgic smells. Two men sat at a table. One had a dark mustache and was clearly a villain. All he needed was a bowl of ice cream he would eat with his fingers. The second man looked like a bartender. His jacket was off. He wore suspenders, and his dark hair was plastered down and parted almost in the middle. He had the face of a dried apple.

"I'm Nitti," he said with a distinct Italian accent. "Talk. Three minutes and then you get out."

I talked fast—about Chico Marx, my friendship with Snorky, the help I needed—but something was wrong. Nitti probably always showed suspicion, but his eyes narrowed to near closing. I took a chance.

"Last and not least," I said, "a guy I met in Miami with Big Al, a guy named Leonardo Bistolfi, got chopped down in my hotel room this morning when I was out."

Nitti eased back. His eyes opened a bit.

"It's good you told about Leonardo," he said. "We knew. We still got a few people who tell us things like that."

He looked about as friendly as he probably could look, so I pushed on

"The cops think maybe you did it," I said, shaking my head as if the very idea was absurd.

Nitti's hands balled into fists and turned from red to white.

"We didn't do it. We don't know who did. We ain't gonna be happy when we find out. Things ain't like when Big Al was here, or Torrio. Johnny kept—" The bad guy with the mustache moved a little and Nitti saw. He cut off his conversation.

"You had your three minutes," said Nitti. "Find your way out."

"But what about help? What about finding Gino?" I said.

Nitti pointed his finger at me and started to get up. The villain with the mustache muttered a calming "Frank," and Nitti sat back and spoke.

"Gino says Marx owes $120,000. He owes it. Big Al asks me to help. I help. Marx has a week to deliver. Understand? I don't like this Chico Marx. Little Jew making fun of Italians. He owes. He pays. Get out. I got other problems."

I was going to say something, but the villain with the mustache turned toward me and shook his head no. I looked at the short fat guy, Lon Chaney, and Nitti, and went.

The fat guy and I went down in the elevator.

"How's Big Al?" he said.

"Nuttier than a fruitcake," I said.

"Yeah," said the fat guy.

Raymond Narducy peered at me over his glasses when I got back into the car.

"You did all right," he said. "You came back with your hair still on."

I let out a King Kong of a sneeze and sat trying to think of what to do next.

"I'm looking for a guy named Gino," I said. "Might be in a place called Cicero. He's got something to do with gambling. Any ideas?"

"Maybe," Narducy mumbled through his scarf. "There's a bar on Wabash, Kitty Kelly's. Guys go there.

Drifters, small timers, some cops and robbers. They got a couple of 21 tables. Used to bet money. Now it's for drinks. A woman who lives in my building works there. Name's Merle Gordon. She might be able to give you a lead."

"Thanks," I said. We headed up west on twenty-second and I did some nasal talking. "I'm a private investigator, not a cop, but you had the rest right. A guy got knocked off in my hotel room. The cops were talking to me about it just before I got in your cab."

Narducy's eyes danced behind his glasses. I went on.

"I'm working for the Marx Brothers. Chico got in some trouble with the mob and—"

"A diabolical concatenation of circumstances," Narducy cried.

"What the hell does that mean?"

"It's from a mystery story. I said it because I just heard on the radio that Chico Marx is in a hospital in Las Vegas."

I slumped back, imagining a fingerless Chico Marx. I'm sure I shuddered, but I wasn't sure whether it was from the cold or my imagination.

"I need ten bucks in change and a telephone," I said.

"Right," said Narducy taking a sudden left. He pulled up to drug store, yanked a leather pouch from under his seat and opened it. It was full of change. He counted out ten bucks. We made the exchange and I ran in the store. There was a wooden phone booth in the back and it was empty.

It took me two minutes to get information and ask

for any Las Vegas radio station. I got the station and asked for the newsroom. The news room turned out to be one man named Almendarez. Almendarez had a nice deep voice. Almendarez told me what hospital Marx was in when I told him I was doing a book on the Marx Brothers and would certainly mention his crucial role in it. My pile of coins was going down, but I had enough left to do plenty. I got the Las Vegas information operator and asked for the right hospital. At the hospital, I said I was Leonard Marx's brother Herbert and that I wanted to talk to my brother.

"Just get his room or whoever is there," I said. "Tell them it's Gummo."

The nurse was undecided, but I said, "Please hurry" and coughed a real cough. She put me through.

Someone picked up the phone, and the nurse said the caller was Gummo Marx and should she put it through. The person on the other end said, "Yes" and it was my turn.

"Hello," I said.

"If you're Gummo," replied the familiar voice of Groucho Marx, "then I'm Andy Hardy. On second thought maybe you're Andy Hardy and I'm Gummo. Whoever you are put the phone down and take a cold bath. I know it does wonders for my dog or my son Arthur. I can't remember which."

I knew he was going to hang up so I shouted, "Wait. My name's Peters. I'm a private detective. Your brother Chico knows me. If he could talk—"

"If he could talk?" chuckled Groucho. "Diamond Jim Marx won't stop talking." He put his hand over the mouthpiece, and I could hear him saying something.

Then another voice came through. It was Chico Marx. I had spoken to him before, but each time I was thrown off by the accent he didn't have. It was so much a part of what I thought Chico Marx was, that I had trouble believing this man with a slight lower East Side accent was the same comic Italian.

"Yeah Peters. What's up?"

"What did they do to you?"

"They? Who?"

"You're in the hospital."

"Nobody did anything to me. I had a heart attack."

"You don't sound like it."

"It wasn't a real heart attack. I'm losing more than I make working in Las Vegas. I checked in here to resist temptation and avoid a few people. Grouch and Harp heard on the radio I was sick and flew here. Harp and me are playing pinochle. I'm losing, but slower than at the tables. Where are you? What did you find out?"

"I'm in Chicago."

"We used to live there. You hear that?" he said to his brothers. "He's in Chicago."

"You stay in that hospital, Chico," I said, dropping another six nickels in the slot to keep from getting cut off by the operator. "The gentlemen here still say you owe them the money, and someone is playing rough. A cheap hood Leonardo got machine gunned in my hotel room."

Groucho must have had his head to the phone listening because he shouted to me.

"Listen to me, Peters. Don't let them add it onto your bill. You didn't order a dead hoodlum and you shouldn't have to pay for one. You should insist that they throw extras like that in free."

Chico took the phone.

"Don't mind him," he said. "He thinks you're one of my friends pulling a gag."

"Well tell him it's no gag. I've got to find Gino. You just stay where you are. I may have to ask you to come to Chicago when I find him. Maybe if he's in the same room with you he'll realize he's got the wrong man."

"And what if he lies and says I'm the right man?" asked Chico.

"Then we break him down, talk a mean streak, or run like hell." I coughed. "I've got no other ideas right now."

"Take care of that cold," said Chico. "Where you staying?"

"The LaSalle," I coughed.

"Harpo says you should gargle with Listerine."

"Tell him thanks, and please stay there till you hear from me." I hung up. Through the window of the phone booth I could see that Narducy had wandered into the drug store. His scarf was off his face. It was a very young face. He waved at me, and I waved back as I got the operator and gave her the number of MGM in Culver City. I told the MGM operator who I was and asked for Louis B. Mayer. She checked and said he was busy, but that Mr. Hoff was to take any calls from me. They put me through.

"Hello Toby," came the voice I recognized. He was a minor vice president at MGM who I had recently helped keep his job—a job he hated.

"Warren," I said, "why is God ducking me?"

"Chico Marx is in the hospital," he said. "Mr.

Mayer thinks it may be because you didn't do what you were paid to do."

"Chico Marx is in a Las Vegas hospital with a fake heart attack," I said truthfully. Then I added not so truthfully, "I told him to go there until I straightened this out. I'm protecting MGM's investment." Post nasal drip got me and I began to cough about ten cents' worth of time.

"Where are you, Toby?"

"Chicago. What's the weather like in L.A.? Wait—don't tell me. Just send me three hundred bucks at the LaSalle Hotel in Chicago and do it fast. I'll itemize it."

"I know," said Warren. "I know," said Warren. "I'll call our district manager in Chicago and have him send the money over in cash. And Toby, the Marx's are talking about quitting the movie business. If they do before you wrap this up, I can give you odds that Mr Mayer is going to fire you with a penny postcard. He's not going to pay to protect an actor who doesn't work for him."

"I guess it makes sense," I coughed.

"Why don't you take some Bromo cold tablets for that cold?" Warren volunteered.

I thanked him for the advice, the money, and the support, and hung up. I marked the cost of the calls in my little book and joined Narducy at the lunch counter.

"I'll buy you lunch, kid," I said with a sneeze. "I'm on top of the world."

"Man on pinnacle has nowhere to step but off," replied Narducy in the most embarrassingly loud Charlie Chan imitation I had ever heard. It was even more embarrassing since we were sitting in a drug store in Chicago's Chinatown and everyone in the place was Chinese but us.

Narducy kept telling the plump Chinese waitress in a yellow uniform that his three burgers were terrific. He asked if they were made with soy sauce. She thought he was funny. I was sick. I drank a bowl of the special soup of the day, tomato, right out of the Heinz can. I also had a large glass of orange juice.

While Narducy considered a fourth burger, I went to the Chinese pharmacist and told him part of my tale—the part about having a bad cold. I hoped he'd come up with an ancient recipe that would cure me. He suggested Bromo Quinine cold tablets. I bought a box of Kleenex instead and gathered up Narducy who, so help me, was amusing the waitress with his Charlie Chan imitation.

"Where to?" he said happily, back in the cab.

"What time's your friend start working at that place you mentioned?"

"Four to midnight. We've got a couple of hours to kill. You want me to spend part of it getting rid of the two guys following us?"

I was proud of myself. I resisted the impluse to turn and look around. I kept my eyes on the back of Narducy's neck, and he kept looking up at the rear view mirror without lifting his head.

"What do they look like?"

"The Phantom of the Opera and Lou Costello. You know 'em?"

"Yeah," I said. "We met at the New Michigan."

"They've got a nice car," said Narducy with sincere admiration. "Big black Caddy."

"That figures," I said. "Lose them, but try not to let them know you're doing it."

He pulled away and made a gentle right down a residentail street past a grade school. Then he made another right and headed back toward what I thought was downtown. His scarf was back over his face and glasses were pushed back on the bridge of his nose indicating, I gathered, that Narducy meant business and business was driving. He went back to Michigan Avenue and headed north, moving just fast enough to pass a few cars in about eight blocks and put four cars between us and them by the time we hit what looked like downtown traffic.

"That's the Art Institute," he said. There were two big green metal lions guarding the stairway of the place. Narducy told me that a few months ago the temperature had dropped below zero, and a kid with a wet hand had stuck to one of the lions. The kid got away with a peeled palm. While he was telling the tale, he increased the distance between us and the comedy team by two more car lengths. After a glance in the mirror, he did a sudden right turn into the open door of a hotel parking garage.

As soon as we were far enough in to be covered by shadow, we both turned to see if we had been spotted. The black car with The Phantom and Costello went by. Narducy did a quick turn and waved away the approaching attendant. With swinging arms and determined inching, Narducy got us back in the direction we had come.

"We're safe," he said proudly.

"Not for long," I said. "All they have to do is call six or seven other guys out on the street to look for your cab. Your big 191 is easy to spot."

"Yeah," he said. "I can catch the details—it's the obvious things that elude me. Well, I guess we say goodbye."

He pulled over and gave me Kitty Kelly's address. It was, he said, about six blocks from where I was standing.

"With a few exceptions, all the streets are straight," he explained. "Each block is a hundred numbers. The streets go by hundreds north and south of Madison Street and west of State. They go east, too, but until you get to the South Side there's not much east. The lake cuts it off. So if the address is 5500 North Western, that means fifty-five blocks north of Madison on Western."

It seemed easy enough. I gave him the meter price

and a two buck tip and entered it in my book.

"See you around," he said. "Say hello to Merle for me."

I walked four blocks, bought a Tribune, and went to a coffee shop. I sipped coffee, nursed my cold, and read slowly, checking the clock. The news hadn't changed much. A Chrysler ad asked me "Why shift gears?" and suggested I get Fluid Drive. Tony Zale the middleweight champ from Gary was going to fight Steve Mamakos in a few hours. Seats were a buck. I wondered if I could risk two or three hours of Chico Marx's and my time and decided I couldn't.

At 3:30 I was getting pushy looks from the waiter. A coffee break crowd was coming in, and I was taking up a table. I paid and went back outside.

A big billboard thermometer said it was twelve degrees above zero. I hurried past a white piece of cake called the Wrigley Building and across a bridge. I wandered in the general direction of where Kitty Kelly's must be. I looked in windows and at theater marquees. It was slightly warmer under the marquees, and there were lots of theaters. A place called the Apollo had *Fantasia*. The Chicago had *Western Union* and Jane Froman on stage. The Roosevel had *High Sierra*. I had seen some of the shooting of that and would have liked to see it, but it was a little after four. I went straight to Kitty Kelly's.

It was a tavern—a little bigger, warmer and darker than most. There were a couple of guys at the bar, and a sign over it saying, "We Only Hire College Girls." a few feet from the bar, a college girl sat on a stool with a little table in front of her. The table was covered in felt, and she was rolling a pile of dice out of a cylinder box.

I walked over to her. She looked up without smiling. I was a dashing figure with my heavy coat turned up at the collar, my hat, ear muffs, red nose, and hand full of toilet paper. She was instantly charmed.

"Twenty-One," she said. "You go under, the drink's free. You go over, you pay double. Care to roll?"

"What college you go to?" I said, leaning forward.

"Stanford," she said without blinking. She was a cute little thing with a serious mouth and short dark hair.

"What did you study?"

"Human Nay-cha," she said in fake Brooklyneese.

I laughed and got caught up in a coughing fit.

"You should do something about that, fella." she said. "Like turning your head away when you get going. I've got a living to make and I don't work on my back."

"That's too bad," I said, recovering enough to talk.

"Hey," she whispered. "You seem like a decent guy. I just got on here and I've got eight hours to go. Don't make this the start of a hard night."

"I won't," I said. "Let's say I lost. What's a beer cost?"

"Twenty-five," she said. "Drop four bits and you're J.P. Morgan."

I dropped fifty cents. She called for a beer from the bartender and asked if I'd carry the beer and my cold to a dark corner.

"You Merle Gordon?" I said, reaching for the beer.

She looked up into my eyes for the first time. Hers were moist and brown and deep.

"You're eyes are like good beer," I said.

"You're a charmer. How'd you know my name."

"Kid named Ray Narducy gave it to me. Said you might be able to help me."

"Do what?" she said suspiciously.

A few more customers came in and moved to the bar. Someone dropped a nickel in the juke box and Dinah Shore sang "I Hear a Rhapsody."

I was a little tired of telling my tale, but I enjoyed leaning toward her and watching her serious face. I went through Capone, the body in the closet, Nitti, and the Marxes.

"You know how many Ginos there must be in and around Chicago?" she said, shaking her head.

"Well," I offered, "we can narrow it down. How many are working for the gangs in gambling?"

"Who knows? Fifteen or twenty. One even comes in here. Gino Amalfitano, but he's not your man. He's in numbers and small. Works the South Side. I'll ask around for you and let you know. Where you staying?"

"The LaSalle," I coughed. "Call me anytime or leave a message."

"You should get in bed alone and take something for that," she sighed with a shake of her head.

I finished off my beer just as Benny Goodman started to play "There'll Be Some Changes Made". I was tired, foot-weary, and out of ideas.

"Hey, wait," she said.

I came back.

"There's a Gino I've heard about who might be your man. Works at a place in Cicero. Private. Gambling. Gino—Gino Servi. It's called the Fireside. And there's—"

"Thanks," I said sincerely and lovingly. "I'll try Servi."

Leonardo Bistolfi's key chain had a disc with "Fireside" enameled on it. It was a possible connection. Even if it fell through, I'd have a good excuse to see Merle Gordon again.

"Tell them Kitty Kelly sent you," she said, throwing the dice again. I bundled up and went back onto Wabash. Above my head the elevated trains made their way around the Loop. I was onto a lead and in love again. All I needed was a new respiratory system.

I walked back to the LaSalle Hotel. It was about five blocks. When I got there, I wasn't in a bad mood. I wasn't in any mood at all. I was weak-kneed and aching.

As soon as I hit the lobby, the desk clerk from the night before recognized me. I had my key in my pocket. I headed for the elevator, but the desk clerk stopped me. I half expected him to wring his hands. He sputtered and stuttered and said Mr. Kotrba, the manager, would like to see me. I said all right and followed him back to the desk. Mr. Kotrba was two hundred pounds of grey, plump pomp and circumstance. He had an extra chin and an angry superiority. He was ready with the wrath of the Lord. I had met dozens of him before. He though he was Hell on a half shell, but he was a pancake. I started in before he could speak.

"Ah, Mr. Kotrba, I was planning to speak to you. Glad I caught you. My company, MGM, called me today and asked me what happened here, suggested I get out of a hotel that allowed murders in the rooms. One of our attorneys, Mr. Leib, even suggested that it would be a good idea to pass the word to people in the other studios to stay away from the LaSalle when they came to Chicago. He even suggested the possibility of a lawsuit because of the emotional distress this has caused me."

Mr. Kotrba's mouth dropped open. I had him backing up and looking for a defense when his original idea had probably been to tell me to get my ass out of his hotel and stop dropping bodies and messing his walls. Kotrba had no flexibility. He was a pushover.

"Don't worry," I said with the best smile I could muster, knowing it would look sardonic. "I talked them out of it, told them the LaSalle was normally a quiet, reasonable place to do business."

"We appreciate that," said Kotrba, patting down wisps of white hair. The desk clerk standing behind him looked mildly amused. He shot me a look of conspiracy which I refused. Whatever his problems with Kotrba, I didn't need a partner.

Before Kotrba could say "But—" I added, "I'm waiting for a special letter from the studio on how I should handle this. Has it arrived?"

The desk clerk stepped forward after pulling something white from the room rack behind him. He handed me an envelope clearly marked with an MGM in the corner. It was, I knew, the $300 Hoff had arranged for.

"Thank you Mr.—"

"Katz," said the clerk, preening. His small mustache glistened. "Curtis Katz."

I opened the envelope without showing its contents. The bills were there. I turned my back on Kotrba whose face now looked white, cold, and a bit dusty like

Chicago snow. My sigh was suitable. I pocked the envelope and turned again.

"They suggest I remain, and the matter be forgotten unless something else happens." I looked straight at Kotrba. This was the moment of truth in which I'd either be in the snow with the beginning of pneumonia or I'd be in a warm room in a few minutes. I could go to another hotel, but that would take time and a bunch of phone calls to tell people what had happened.

"We're very pleased to hear that," Kotrba sighed with relief.

"Good," I said. "Send a boy up to my room in five minutes for my suit. I want it cleaned and pressed, fast."

"Of course," said Kotrba, "and if there's anything we can do, please let Mr. Katz know."

I went up the elevator and into my room. With the door open, I checked the bathroom, under the bed and in the closet. There were no bullies or bodies. I locked and double bolted the door, took off my suit, hung it on a hanger, and started running a hot bath while I made a few calls.

First I called Kleinhans. It was after six, and he was out getting a sandwich. Then I called my office in Los Angeles. It was just after four there, and Shelly Minck should still be in. He was.

"Toby" he shouted, ever distrustful of the ability of the phone company to transmit voices outside the circumference of Los Angeles County. "I'm glad you called. Remember Mr. Stange?"

Mr. Stange was a neighborhood bum Shelly had pulled out from under the stairs in our office building.

Mr. Stange had only one tooth. Shelly had dedicated himself to saving that denture and anchoring a new personality to it.

"I remember Mr. Stange."

"We saved the tooth. There's a slight infection, but nothing serious."

Shelly's office, hands, and body were a hymn to decay. His only defense against rampant infection was the cigar he held in his mouth even when working on patients. He was enough to make Lister and Semmelweis commit murder or resign from the health game.

"Shelly, do I have any mail or messages?"

"I'll go check. It rained here."

"Too bad," I said. "It's beautiful here in Chicago." Through the window I could see that the darkness was complete. It had been almost dark before five o'clock. Shelly grunted and went for my mail.

"Let's see. Looks like a bill, some ads, a letter that smells very nice. Want me to open it?"

"Who's it from?"

"Ann Peters with a return address of—"

"I know the address."

"Want me to open it?"

"No," I said. Someone knocked at the door. "Leave it on my desk. I'll be back in a few days, I think."

"Right. I've got a bridge to build for Mr. Stange. Want me to wait till you get back?" Someone knocked again.

"No," I said. "Science will have to move on without my admiration. Goodbye."

I hung up and went to the door. I was curious about why my ex-wife would write to me. The last time I had seen her she made it clear that I wasn't welcome company, and she was seriously thinking about marrying some guy at the airline she worked for. Whatever she wanted, I didn't want it filtered through Shelly Minck.

The "kid" at the door was about seventy. He took my suit and said he'd have it back in an hour. I got in a hot bath, letting myself cough and sputter. After my suit came back and I had tipped the old kid fifty cents, I lay down on the bed in the dark in clean underwear and listened to "Information Please," "Gang Busters" and "The Adventures of Sherlock Holmes." Both Warden Lawes and Holmes got the guy they were after. It inspired me to rise out of bed and begin the search for Gino Servi. I flicked off the radio two minutes into Lawrence Welk from the Trianon Ballroom, put on my suit and coat and went down in the lobby. I didn't take the gun. I'd never used it, and the place I was going there were probably a lot of people who would recognize that bulge and not take kindly to it.

I waved to Curtis Katz at the desk and asked the doorman to get me a cab. One was waiting about twenty feet away. The life of semiluxury felt good, but I started to worry. I knew what I was going back to when this was over. I didn't want to get too used to things I couldn't have.

While I pondered the meaning of life, gobbled Bromo Quinine cold tablets, and blew my nose into Kleenex, the cab driver pulled quietly into the Chicago night.

When I told the cabbie I wanted to go to the Fireside Lounge in Cicero, he turned to look at me and shrugged. We arrived in front of the place half an hour later. He took my fare and tip and shook his head sadly.

When I got out, I was facing a black Cadillac parked across the street. The guy behind the wheel looked like Lon Chaney. His eyes were pointed straight at me.

There were at least two possibilities. One was that Nitti's two boys, with some help from Nitti's friends on the police force, had found out I was staying at the LaSalle and had simply waited and followed the cab when I came out. Another possibility was that Gino Servi was the man I wanted, and they had simply waited for me to show up in Cicero, which would suggest they had more confidence in my detecting that I did. Of course their presence could have been a coincidence. I'd heard that you could safely stand on a streetcorner in Cicero forever and never see anyone you knew. That's what I'd heard, but it was old information from an ex-con named Red. The thing that mattered was that Nitti's men knew where I was. I tried not to think about what they wanted from me.

Cicero was no warmer than Chicago, and in spite of its name, the Fireside did not look particularly warm. It was a big fake-log building with a gravel-covered parking lot you got in by driving under a sign on hinges. It was too dark to tell if the logs were brown. The windows were covered with dark drapes and a small red neon sign over the door announced the location. The large *F* in the sign flickered and threatened to give up. When it did, the *ireside* would be in business.

I went through the heavy wooden door, dragging flu-stricken legs, and found myself facing another door with a menu on it. All items on the bill of fare had been crossed off. That and the lack of prices didn't encourage the dinner trade.

Through a second door I found a creature who looked something like a juke box—short, solid, and wearing a maroon jacket and tie. The dim light turned his face orange and purple and danced on glasses so thick they looked bulletproof.

"Kitty Kelly sent me," I said.

He put his newspaper aside, looked me over. He made it clear that it didn't matter who sent me. I wasn't carrying hardware. That was all he cared about. His job was to send them in, not keep them out. He took my coat and handed it through a dark square. Something or somebody inside the dark square took it.

"Go on in," said the juke box, with a slight Irish accent. I went on in, stifling a sniffle.

"In" was a large, softly lit, low-ceilinged room with no fireplace. "In" did not look particularly warm. There were about sixty men and women in the room, well to reasonably dressed, at five card tables and a roulette wheel. One-armed bandits lined the walls and jingled constantly. There was a bar in the right corner with a door behind it. The bar was so small that only a half dozen stools were needed to surround it. Patrons apparently were not encouraged just to drink and pass the time of day with Joe the bartender, who looked like he was eight feet tall and not the kind of guy you'd want to pass any time with, or meet by chance in the washroom.

A single pillar, about as big around as a small redwood, stood in the middle of the room, but it wasn't supporting the ceiling. I'd seen pillars like this in Vegas and Reno. The pillar had an eye-level series of dark mirrors running around it. Inside the pillar was at least one man with a gun, probably a very big gun. There was no real attempt to hide the purpose of the pillar. The door was clearly outlined and was surely locked on the inside. If the man with the gun had a heart attack, it would probably take dynamite to get to him. I had the feeling that dynamite might not be too far away either. The pillar was a warning to youthful, ambitious punks who might want to take on the power. It was also a reassurance to the honest patrons and an extra eye on the possibly dishonest ones.

A platinum blonde moved away from a pair of youngish women at the bar and headed for me. She wore a black dress that glittered in the soft brown light. She was about forty, maybe a little skinny, with a good smile and a voice the suggested a touch of state college.

"Companionship, or action?" she said.

Our eyes met. I wondered how long and deep-someone would have to scratch, and with what, to get through her first three lines of defense. From the way she looked at me, I could see that I didn't have the tools for the job. Maybe it was my running nose and rheumy eyes.

"I'm here from out of town," I said, trying to look the part. My red nose probably helped the Mortimer Snerd image. "I'd like to try my luck at that roulette table."

I rubbed my hands together, not hard enough to start a fire but enough to show I was hot to lose the few bucks I had saved in a sock in the old chicken coop.

"Oh brother," she said, grinning and taking my arm. My first level of disguise had certainly been penetrated. I had been taken for a clown instead of an idiot.

She guided me around black jack and poker tables to the roulette wheel in the far left corner.

"We work in chips," she whispered. "Fives, tens, twenties and fifties. You pay me, and I give the chips. You turn in what you have, if anything, when you leave. I usually get a tip."

"I'll start with fifty bucks in fives," I said. I counted out fifty-five and shook the last five indicating it was a tip. Her mask grin stayed put. Instead of sitting at the table, I watched her walk to the bartender, who took the cash and handed her the chips. The barkeep immediately took my money through the door behind the bar.

The blonde came back, gave me ten white chips, patted my shoulder and said, "Find me if you need more chips. The guys in red are the waiters. Just call them if you want to order a drink. You can pay them in cash or chips."

There were seven or eight players at the roulette table. The first thing I noticed was the croupier, who never smiled and whose voice mever changed. He was a thin guy with a tux and a little mustache. As the night wore on, his French accent disappeared.

I squeezed in next to a tall, lean guy in his early thirties, wearing a perfectly tailored suit with a neat white monogrammed handkerchief in the pocket. He smoked his cigarette in a pearl holder and seemed slightly amused by the table, which didn't look in the least funny to me.

"How you doing?" I said, pushing a white chip on the black.

The lean guy looked at me with a raised eyebrow and answered with an upper crust English accent that seemed somehow wrong for Cicero.

"I'm losing," he said, "but through my losses I'm developing a plan. All it takes is money and a great deal of patience."

He lost his red chip and I lost my white one.

"You have enough money and patience?" I sniffled.

"A reasonable supply of the former and an almost infinite supply of the latter. Fortunately, I'm obsessed with the Romantic fantasy that I will someday break the bank and save the British Empire."

We both lost again. He didn't appear to mind. I decided he was imitating George Sanders playing a cad, or maybe George Sanders imitated this guy when he played a cad. English's superior sneer seemed permanently fixed under a once broken nose, which added a soldier-of-fortune air to his good looking long face.

My next monumental sneeze raised a grumble from a be-ringed matron on my right. I blew my nose and lost five bucks more in atonement. English raised his right hand elegantly, and a waiter who had been stuffed into a maroon jacket two sizes too small galloped over on the dark tile floor. The slot machines provided his musical accompaniment.

"Have you a halfway decent wine?" English asked him, making clear what he expected the answer to be by the doubting arch of his brow.

"Yeah," said the waiter, confirming his assumption.

English handed the waiter a white chip and told him to bring a glass of wine, preferable something French from the Loire, with a glass of orange juice and a raw egg.

The waiter said, "Right," and walked away. English leaned over to me.

"He'll come back with Chianti," he said, losing ten bucks more on number seven.

I skipped a couple of spins and looked around the room for someone who might be Gino or for Nitti's men. If Gino was there, I decided, he was behind that door on the other side of the bar. Even if I could make it past the enormous barkeep, I had a feeling things were behind that door that could cause me grief.

The wine, juice, and egg arrived. English held the dark glass to his nose and frowned.

"California, no more than a year old," he sighed. "But it will have to do. Actually it has to be swallowed quickly, so it doesn't matter if there's nothing to savor."

With all eyes on him including that of the croupier,

he cracked the egg into the juice. Instead of drinking the contents of the two glasses, he handed them to me.

"Gulp it down like a good lad," he said around his cigarette holder. "Then bolt down the wine."

I raised a hand to protest, and hit the matron, who countered with a sharp push on my back. English guided the drinks into my hand. I drank them. What the hell. I couldn't feel much worse than I did.

"Five minutes, you'll be able to take on a orangutang," he said, returning to his bet.

"I may have to," I replied, wiping orange juice from my mouth with a table napkin.

He looked at me archly, and after ordering a Bourbon and branch water went on with his determined march to backruptcy.

In five minutes I felt much better and had lost my fifty bucks in chips. I waved to the blonde, who walked over to me, lighting the way with her capped teeth. When she leaned, I gave her another fifty, wondering how I'd get the money back from Louis B. Mayer.

"I'd like to talk to Gino," I whispered.

"Gino who?"

"Gino Servi."

Who are you?" she said.

"Tell him a friend of Chico's."

"I'll see if this Gino is around." She never lost her smile.

English regarded me with exaggerated new respect. I was about ten years older than he was, but he made me feel like a kid.

"That was very nice," he said, pulling in his first

win since I had sat down. "Sounded a little like something out of *Little Caesar*."

"More like *Dead End*," I answered, pushing a chip forward on the red. For the next twenty minutes, I began to lose more slowly, which I considered a major moral triumph. The platinum lady came back and whispered to me.

"Gino will see you at closing time. Three o'clock, if you want to stick around."

I said I would. My watch told me I had a couple hours to kill, and my wallet told me I'd never make it at the present rate. I started to spend my money on wine, eggs, and juice, drank the wine more slowly, and managed to lose a hundred and fifty bucks while I learned some things about English. We were quite a pair. He was upper class with a few generations of a lot of money. My old man had been a small Glendale grocer who left my brother and me a pile of debts when he died. English had been educated in Europe. I had missed finishing my second year in junior college when I joined the Glendale cops. He knew his way around the world. I knew Los Angeles County and about a hundred miles around it.

When the dials under the scratched lens of my trusty watch told me it was almost time, my cold was under temporary and artificial control. By a quarter to three, there was no one in the place except Joe the bartender and me, the platinum lady, the English guy, and the cleanup crew.

The blonde told English it was closing time. He threw the croupier a red chip, handed the blonde his remaining chips to cash in, downed his Bourbon and branch water, and spoke softly to me.

"Give you a lift?"

"I'm going back to downtown Chicago, but I may be tied up here for a few minutes."

"No trouble," he said. "I'm going that way. I'll just wait right outside for you."

The blonde brought him his cash, his coat, and a goodby smile. Two minutes later I was alone with the cleaning staff of the Fireside. Ten minutes after that I was just alone. Someone turned off the lights except for a few over the bar and night lights in each corner. The long white shadows out of darkness were great for my nerves.

There was a noise at the pillar. It opened and a man in a white shirt and no jacket came out. His shirt was wrinkled with sweat, and his hair was plastered down from oil or the steam bath of the inside of that pillar. He walked over to the exit door and casually leaned against it. The door opened and the man who looked like a juke box came in, peered around the room with his head forward, found me, cleaned his glasses on his sleeve, and stood on the other side of the exit door. Outside a car went by with a loose gasket and a drunken kid yelled, "Yahh!"

A few seconds later the door behind the bar opened and three figures came out, outlined in strong light behind them. They closed the door and disappeared in the darkness near the bar. My irises kicked back, and I saw two of the men were the familiar winners of the Lon Chaney and Lou Costello look-alike contest. The third

guy was the mustached villain from Nitti's room in the
New Michigan Hotel.

"You Gino Servi?" I asked. My voice took a half
bounce back off the walls. No answer. The five men
looked at me as if I were a dog act about to begin.

"You should have left town this morning," said
Servi. "You don't get two chances." Servi went back
through the door behind the bar.

"Hey, wait—" I yelled. "Let's talk. I've—"

He was gone.

My best hope was that the quartet had not been
told to kill me, just have a little fun and send me on my
way in my underwear with an hour to get out of town. I
could either take what they were planning for me or try
to get out. With both doors covered, my chances for
escape were less than that of Mamkos against Zale.

"O.K.," I said, putting up my palms and chuckling.
"You win. I'm going. Give me time to get my suitcase
and I'll be gone. A man should know when he's
beaten."

At one level of consciousness, I told whatever gods
may be that I would get out of town if I had the chance.
At another level, I knew that if I got out of here I wasn't
leaving town. But there really wasn't any issue or debate. The four horsemen weren't having any.

"I travel light," I said.

"You don't travel anymore," said Costello, stepping forward. "You get a long rest."

Chaney started to move toward me from the left, a
phantom in the shadows. The juke box man and the
guy from the pillar just watched. They were back-up

men and probably wouldn't be needed against the likes of me.

"I've had too much rest recently," I said, backing away. Costello was coming at me slowly. I said a few more things, but I don't remember what they were. What I wanted was for Costello to keep coming forward while I backed away, to get him off balance and somehow get past him and make a run for the door behind the bar. There wasn't much chance I'd make it, but no one had a better idea. I backed into a card table, babbled something, and put everything I had into a right to Costello's face. He staggered with the punch, but didn't give me room to get by on his right. Chaney was blocking the left. Costello's face came into a patch of light. He was smiling in a way I did not like, and a thin line of blood trickled from his left nostril to his mouth. I pulled back for another swing, but Chaney caught me with an underhand right to my gut. I flew back, gasping for air, and bounced over the black-jack table behind me. The table went over, sending cards, ash trays, and an unfinished drink flying into the dark.

I was on my back when they reached me. Somebody pulled me to my knees. Somebody else got a good grip on my hair and held my head up. The next move would be a fist in my face. Nausea hit me first, and I tried to see if the leveling fist held a glint of metal.

The knock at the door was sharp and hard. It broke through shadows and split the smoke-filled shafts of light in the hidden corners of the room and my mind. The five of us froze, staring at the door. The knock came again, followed by a cheery English voice.

"Hello in there. I'm afraid I've forgotten something

rather important in there. Mind opening up for a moment?"

A thick palm smelling like garlic, urine, and tobacco covered my mouth.

"Come now," said English. "I hear you in there and I simply must have what I left. It's quite valuable. I'd dislike my alternative, but if I do not get in I'll have to solicit the aid of the police."

"Let him in," croaked Costello.

The juke box man turned, slid the bolt and opened the door. English walked in, carrying his coat. He squinted into the darkness. When his eyes adjusted, he saw me.

"Ah, there you are. Heard the noise and thought you might be in some need of aid."

I managed a *grummph* through Costello's fingers.

"Sorry," English said to Costello. "I really can't make out what he's saying. Could you remove your hand from his face?"

"Get out of here," grunted Costello. "And forget what you see. That's good advice."

English scratched his head.

"Sorry, again, but that just wouldn't be possible."

The juke box man had moved behind English and had his arms out waiting for the signal from Costello. I couldn't warn him, but he didn't need my warning. English's left elbow shot back blind, catching the juke box just below the rib cage. While he bellowed in pain, English spun around, pulled the man's glasses off and threw his coat over the guy in the sweaty white shirt. He punched at the covered head and the coat and man went down.

Costello let go of me and made a rush at English, while Chaney reached in his jacket. I caught Chaney around the knees, and he went down with me on top of him, aiming a fist in the general direction of his face. Costello moved low with his arms out like a wrestler. English met him straight up with his right hand out. He moved out of the path of the rush and grabbed for Costello's hair, but there wasn't any. Costello caught English in the stomach with his head, but English was backing away from the awkward turn and used the heavier man's move forward to pull him off balance by grabbing his collar. Costello went sailing in a midair somersault and hit the tile floor with a thud that shook the room. The whole thing couldn't have taken more than a few seconds. My wind was back and I was still on top of Chaney, who was hitting me in the side and head with wide punches that must have been hell on his knuckles and were doing my head no good at all.

White Shirt had the coat off his head and was going for his holster. I saw him. English saw him too, but we weren't close enough to do anything about it, and neither of us had a gun. A rush would bring a bullet through the top of one of our skulls. English pulled out his fountain pen. Maybe he knew it was the end and was going to write a quick will or down a small supply of Bourbon and branch water hidden in the pen's bladder.

I was on my feet ready for a heroic rush at White Shirt, whose gun was just coming out, when something popped in the Englishman's fountain pen and a thin blast of what looked like steam and liquid hit White Shirt in the face. By the time I had taken two steps, White Shirt was choking in pain with his hands covering his face. I was near enough so some of the gas made me feel clammy and a little sick. Unable to see, White Shirt let loose with a couple of wild shots in our direction. One of them hit Costello, who was in a sitting position a dozen feet away. His right hand went to his shoulder and he yowled.

With his neat handkerchief over his mouth, the Englishman walked up to White Shirt and hit his gun hand with an open palm. The gun skidded across the floor and let out another protest shot on its own. The shot cracked the metal hide of a slot machine, sending it berserk.

"Think that's about it, don't you?" said English, putting his handkerchief back in his pocket and picking up his coat. He seemed in no hurry, but I was. Somewhere in the dark, Chaney was probably on his hands and knees reaching for his gun.

We stepped over the juke box man's groaning body, went through the two doors and into the night. I was sweating. The cold air hit me like dry ice. English pointed to a small foreign car right at the door, and I hurried in. My coat was on the seat.

When he had gotten in his side slowly and straightened his coat, he lit a cigarette, placed it in his pearl holder, and explained, "Only coat left. I assumed it must be yours."

"It is," I said, throwing a look at the door of the Fireside. Chaney staggered out into the cold, looked our way and lifted his gun. English glanced at him casually and pulled away, kicking up gravel as a bullet spat through the side window a foot from his head. He didn't seem to notice. We were out of range when the second shot came.

"Now," he said with a smile. "Where am I to take you?"

"LaSalle Hotel on LaSalle as fast as you can get there. I'd better check out and find someplace safer. Thanks for what you did back there."

"My pleasure," he grinned, raising an eyebrow.

"You were pretty cool."

"Was I?" he said happily. "I was petrified. Never did anything like that before, but it doesn't do to let the enemy know, and it was damned exhilarating, wasn't it?"

The way back was through Cicero and the South Side of Chicago, with the sun just thinking about coming up. We sped past low wooden homes with early morning smoke coming from their brick chimneys and heavy-faced men with lunch pails waiting for streetcars. I watched and told English my tale of Hollywood, Capone, the Marx Brothers, and the Nitti acting society.

I said it had all been great fun and told him some of my other fun in the private detective business. We exchanged further tales. My tale was something out of Dime Detective. The story he told sounded like *Beau Geste*.

He was the second of three brothers from a rich banking family. His father had been a member of Parliament and had been killed in the last war. His mother had sent him to Eton, where he had been a pretty fair athlete and had broken his nose in a soccer game. Then things had gone downhill. He was booted out of a place called Sandhurst for chasing girls and sent someplace in the Austrian mountains where he found more girls, learned German, French, and Russian, and took up skiing.

Then he moved on to a short shot at banking, gave up, became a reporter, and found his calling just when England went to war with Germany. He had been recruited by British Naval Intelligence and was now a Lieutenant in the Special Branch of the Royal Naval Volunteers. At present he was stationed someplace in Canada he couldn't tell me about.

He pulled up next to the LaSalle. Before getting out, I struggled into my coat and looked around for a waiting car or suspicious face. I saw none. I opened the door and reached over to shake English's hand.

"My name's Peters," I said, "Toby Peters."

"Good to meet you Toby Peters," he said. "I'm staying at the Ambassador if you need someone to share any further adventures. My name's Ian Fleming."

There was no one in the LaSalle Hotel lobby except a drowsing bellhop whose uniform buttons needed polishing. Curtis Katz was at the desk looking just slightly wilted at the end of an all-night shift. He gave me the hint of a smile.

"I'm checking out," I said. "Get my bill ready. I'll be right down."

"I hope it wasn't—"

No," I said, hurrying to the elevator. "Urgent business back in Hollywood. Gable needs me. You know how it is."

Katz knew how it was. The elevator boy put his newspaper down and brought me up to six. By the time I reached my door, the power of Ian Fleming's elixir had just about worn off. I turned the key and kicked the door open with my foot. No one shot at me. I switched on the light, did a quick check of the bathroom and closet, put on my hoster and .38, and snapped one of the locks of my suitcase (the other was broken when I bought it). Since I had never unpacked, the whole process took me about two minutes.

I paid Katz with a check when I got back to the lobby. My account in L.A. might just barely cover it, and I couldn't afford to give up any cash. I was heading for the door when Katz called, "Wait."

"Yes?" I said nervously, looking down through the pattern of scratches on my watch, to show I was in a hurry.

"You have a message." He got the message while I watched the entrance doors for a familiar face with a machine gun under it.

"Mr. Marx called from La Vegas," preened Katz. "Said he and his brothers would arrive at Midway Airport here at noon. I presumed you'd know who Mr. Marx was."

"I do know, Curtis," I said, leaning over the counter confidentially. "I can call you Curtis, can't I?"

"Certainly," he smiled.

"Good," I beamed back. "Mr. Marx is a producer. We're thinking of shooting a movie with Gable here in Chicago. It's important that no one know Mr. Marx is in town. So if anyone comes looking for me, don't give them the information. Might be reporters or a rival studio. You know how those things are?"

He knew how those things were. I strongly suggested that his cooperation would be borne in mind when the decision was made to shoot the picture.

There would be good jobs and small roles for friends.

There were no cabs around, and the morning sun was already high enough by now to keep the streets from having any good shadows to jump into. There were some people on the streets, probably hotel workers, pickpockets, and confused drunks who had lost their way. I didn't think the presence of a few people would stop Nitti's friends from gunning me down on LaSalle Street.

I ran across the street. My suitcase bounced as if it was about to split, and my holster and gun put a weight on my chest I didn't like. I pushed through the nearest revolving door.

Stepping back into the lobby of an office building, I watched a familiar big black Cadillac pull up in front of the LaSalle. Two men jumped out. One was Costello, with his right arm in a sling. The other was the juke box man. Chaney was at the wheel of the car. He looked right at the building I was in, but I was sure the lobby was dark enough.

Two things had probably given me the time to get out of the LaSalle. I had hoped for one or both and had been rewarded. Costello was whatever brains the group of muscle had, and he didn't have much. He didn't want to call Nitti or Servi and tell them that I got away if he didn't have to. He probably could have put in a call and had someone waiting for me when Fleming and I drove up at the LaSalle, but Costello was counting on getting me without help and without admitting a failure. He had also stopped to get his arm bandaged and put in a sling.

Costello ran into the LaSalle and came back out in

less than two minutes. He didn't look as if he had found out much if anything from Katz. Before he got back in the car, he looked around the street, but he didn't see me or anything else of interest. I gave them three more minutes to get out of the neighborhood and made a dash for a taxi that pulled up in front of the LaSalle to let someone out.

"Midway Airport," I told the cabbie. On the way, I considered the possibility that Costello might call Nitti and they might have a couple of people at airports and train stations to stop me from leaving. Then I figured that Nitti probably wouldn't bother. He hadn't been kicked around by a middle-aged detective and a stylish Englishman. Nitti would probably be happy to have me get out of town. Costello and his chums might think otherwise, but they'd have to report to Servi or Nitti before too much time passed, or risk their own heads on the train tracks.

The trip to Midway was long. I blew my nose a few times, dozed off a few more times, and ignored the driver. When we got to the airport, I paid him off and hurried inside. I found a washroom, shaved, and changed my shirt. Then I found a coffee shop, had some Wheaties with sliced bananas, and bought a newspaper.

I found the waiting room where the Marx Brothers flight would come in, but I was hours early. I took a seat in the middle of a group of guys who looked like businessmen and were talking about options.

The paper told me it was Saturday. It also told me that snow would fall, that five senators didn't like some war bill, and that slot machines were running wide open in the northern suburbs of Cook County. I could have shown them a few in the western suburb of Cicero, too. I also found out that British raiders had bombed Nazi bases in Sicily. That wasn't what I was looking for. I paused over a story of some kids in Sag Harbor, New York, at a place called Pierson High School. Some of the students had dressed up as storm troopers and started to bully others to show how it feels. There was a picture with the story, showing some girls scrubbing a sidewalk with the young storm troopers standing over them. J. Edgar Hoover was asking for seven hundred more FBI men to help curb Nazi spies. Then I found what I was looking for. Tony Zale had KO'd Mamkos in the fourteenth. Zale had gone down in the fifth, and the fight had been close up until the knockout.

Content, I fell asleep. My dream was about men with different mustaches, all leering and chasing me around a gym. There was a Groucho mustache, a Servi mustache, a Katz mustache, a Hitler mustache. I started throwing balls and gradually worked my way up through baseballs, basketballs and medicine balls. None of them stopped the attack, and my old pal Koko didn't materialize to save me. I ran through a door and found myself in downtown Cincinnati. I woke up with a groan and a massive sneeze. No one was sitting next to me. I had just enough time to lug my suitcase to a newsstand, buy some aspirin, gulp down a half dozen, and make it back to the waiting room when the Las Vegas plane came in.

Nobody looking like Marx Brothers came off in the first batch. I was about to give up when I heard the familiar screen voice of Groucho saying,

"The least Perry Mason could have done was meet us here."

The voice came out of a short, erect dark man with a decidedly Jewish face. He was flanked by two slightly older men his own size who looked like twins. I stepped in front of the three men and spoke to one of the twins.

"Chico Marx?" I tried.

"That's Harpo," said Groucho. "And it's pronounced *Chick-o*, because he's a chick chaser. Well, whoever you are, you didn't waste any time in trying to sell us brushes." He looked down at my suitcase.

"I'm Peters," I said.

"We're Wheeler and Zoolsey and El Brendel," said Groucho, whose bad mood was spreading beyond the four of us.

"I'm Chico,"said one of the men who looked like twins. He held out his hand and I took it. "These are my brothers, Groucho and Harpo."

"Our real names are Julius, Leonard and Arthur," said Groucho, "but the last person who called us that is still locked in the bathroom of Loew's State."

Clumps of people went past us, but no one gave even the hint of recognizing the famous brothers. I would have missed them myself if I hadn't heard Groucho's voice. Chico's voice, as I knew, was nothing like his screen voice.

An idea hit me, but I needed time to put it together.

"Well," said Groucho, "are you going to erect a tent so we can have a noon tea, or are we going to get off of this elephant path?"

I led them to the coffee shop. While they ordered lunch, I did some fast explaining, giving the whole story of the search for Servi, and Nitti's refusal to listen.

"So, you're telling us Chico should pay $120,000 he doesn't owe," said Groucho.

"No," I said.

"I see, I see," said Groucho. "You're telling us Chico shouldn't pay and should wait until somebody with a pushed-in face—no offense—"

"None taken," I said.

"Some guy with a pushed-in face," Groucho went on, "turns him into Swiss cheese."

"No," I said.

"You're a sterling judge of options, Peters," said Groucho, turning his attention to a chicken sandwich. "And I'd like to sit around this Chicago version of Ciro's for days, but we've got to throw ourselves on the mercy of someone fast. Just lead us to this Servi character and we'll work something out."

"Now wait a minute, Grouch," said Chico quietly, while Harpo ate silently with eyes never leaving his brothers. "Maybe Toby has a plan."

"I've got a plan," said Groucho. "You sign legal papers turning all your earnings over to me so things like this don't happen again. You've gambled away more money than you've earned, and that's a lot of gambling."

"Come on, Grouch," sighed Chico. "We gonna go through that again?"

"No, no. Sorry to bring it up and ruin your lunch. Just pretend I didn't say anything. We'll just go on forever making movies so you can keep ahead of your debts. We're middle-aged men. We should be bouncing grandchildren and planting petunias. Instead we run around getting hit by trains, falling off horses, and getting punched by heavies."

It sounded like my life. I let them talk for a few more minutes while I ate an egg sandwich. The three of them had obviously been through this so many times that they knew the routine. Harpo apparently wanted no part of it.

"O.K., Peters," sighed Groucho, finishing off his sandwich. "What's your plan—though I know I shouldn't ask."

"The three of you go to a hotel," I said. "You know any hotels in Chicago?"

"We used to live here back in the vaudeville days," said Chico. "We know the town. How about the Palmer House? There's usually a good card game or two."

"This is against my better judgment, but we'll be at the Drake," said Groucho.

"And," I went on. "Don't register with your own names."

"I almost never do," said Groucho, "but then again, it's not because I'm hiding with my brothers. We'll give you two days for your plan."

"Fair enough. You sit tight and don't call anybody. I've got an idea that may get you out of this, but it will take me a day or so to set it up."

"Right," said Chico. "We can play pinochle in our rooms."

"I didn't even bring my guitar," sighed Groucho.

We picked up their bags and caught a cab. On the way back, I asked them if they were ever spotted on the street and asked for autographs. They agreed that they weren't very often. I was fairly sure that if I didn't know who they were and couldn't tell Chico from Harpo at first look, it might not be bery difficult for some small, Jewish-looking guy to pass himself off as the real Chico Marx. It was a wacky possibility, but it was worth a try and it gave me something to work on. First, find the guy who passed for Chico, if such a guy existed. Second, set up a meeting with Chico and Servi, so Servi could either lie or say Chico was the wrong guy. The second was dangerous for Chico, but things didn't look too great for him now. I didn't know how to go about the first.

After I checked the brothers in at the Drake—as the Rothsteins of Ohio—I headed for a telephone and called Sergeant Kleinhans. It took a while to track him down.

"Where are you, Peters?" he said. "You checked out of the LaSalle."

"Some friends of Frank Nitti were looking for me," I said. "I've got some news and questions. You want to hear them or do you want to threaten me?"

"Both," he said. "What have you got?"

"The guy who put the finger on Chico is Gino Servi. Know him?"

"Yep. Keep going."

"There's a good chance that if Servi sees Chico Marx, he'll know he's the wrong man. Servi doesn't like me, but I"ll give it a try."

"You're going to bring Chico Marx here for that?" said Kleinhans.

"I can get him if I have to," I said. "The second

possibility is to find someone who might have passed himself off as Chico Marx. He doesn't have to look just like him, maybe wasn't even gambling before. He might have a record. Between forty or fifty-five or so. Short."

"That's nothing to go on," said Kleinhans. "But I'll fish around. Where can I reach you?"

"You can't. I'll call you back. People in the Chicago police department are on Nitti's payroll. They knew I was at the LaSalle and about the murder of Bistolfi before you did."

Kleinhans laughed.

"Tell me something new," he said. "O.K. Give me a call."

I hung up, picked up my suitcase, went to the bar, ordered a Fleming flu special, and went outside to call a cab. I told the cabbie to take me to Kitty Kelly's. There wasn't a safe hotel for me in Chicago, and my friendships were nonexistent.

Suitcase in hand and collar up, I slouched into Kitty Kelly's. Before my eyes adjusted to the dark, I blew my nose and did a little play with my coat buttons. Then I made out forms at the bar and the three Twenty-One tables. Merle Gordon was at the same table where I had seen her before.

"You don't look so good," she volunteered.

"I've been sick," I sighed.

She rolled the dice and motioned me closer.

"Drop a quarter, pretend you've lost, and get the hell out of here," she whispered. I tried to look down the top of her dress. She caught me, but I hadn't been trying to hide it. She shook her head and grinned.

"You're something," she said. "You mentioned

Kitty Kelly's to get into the Fireside last night. Somebody remembered and came here asking about you."

"Stumpy guy with a sling?" I guessed.

"Right," she answered, rolling the dice. "I told him I didn't know anybody who looked like you and no one else here remembered you, but one of the other girls might notice you right now. So goodbye, and it's been nice knowing you."

I didn't move.

"Nowhere to go," I said. "Can't check into a hotel. The bad guys might have them covered, and I don't know many people in Chicago."

My eyes went down. I tried to look near defeat, shoulders slumped, eyes moist. Years ago it had worked on my wife Anne, but the last time I tried it on her she wasn't having any. She had had enough of mothering me.

Merle pulled a pad of paper from under the table and scribbled on it. Then she reached deeper under the table and came up with something that tinkled.

"Reach over and take these," she said. "And drop another quarter. My address is on the note and that's the key. There's juice in the refrigerator. Sleep on the sofa. I'll be there later. I'm off early today."

I grinned.

"Forget it," she said. "You stay on that sofa and away from me. I can't afford to catch your cold."

I shrugged with enormous regret, pocketed key and note, and went outside to find a cab.

Merle's apartment was a little north of the Loop, on a street called Barry. It was a three-story yellow building with a courtyard and maybe twenty apartments in three entrances. Her place was in the second entrance on the second floor. It was small—two rooms with a kitchen area that stood in a corner of the living room. The bedroom was big enough for a single bed. On the chest of drawers near the bed, there was a picture of a good-looking man with a thin smile. The picture looked as if it were a few years old. There was also a picture of a little girl—a cute kid with dark hair, a big grin, and a tooth missing in front. She looked something like Merle.

The furniture looked used or rented. It was clean, but it didn't look like the kind of thing I would have guessed she had. The refrigerator had a full quart of juice. I drank most of it and looked for cereal while I made coffee. There wasn't any cereal, so I ate a sandwich with two slices of something that was either pale salami or ripe bologna. There was no bath, just a shower. I used it, shaved, drank my coffee, and stretched out on the sofa with a roll of toilet paper for my nose. I fell asleep. No dreams came. No trip to Cincinnati. No Marx Brothers.

A knock at the door pulled me slowly out of the sofa. I fumbled for my gun and tried not to breathe, which is easy with a deviated septum and the flu. I had figured Merle for someone who'd help a poor bedraggled detective, but I've been wrong about women, men and kids all my life. She might just have given Costello a call, claimed a reward or amnesty, and gone back to the dice.

"Wake up and open the door," she whispered. "You took my only key."

I opened the door, holding the gun behind my back. She came in and threw her coat on a chair.

"You always sleep with that?" she said, walking to the kitchen.

"This," I said looking at the gun. "I don't know what this is."

She touched the coffee, found it cold and turned the heat back on. Then she turned and looked at me. I had taken my clothes off and stood in underwear and a tee shirt with the .38 in my hand. I looked down at myself and shrugged. She laughed and drank her coffee.

"You alone?"

"Peters," I said. "Toby Peters. If you mean do I have a family, just a brother. Nothing else. I once had a wife."

"I know how that is," she said, biting her lower lip.

"You want to talk about it?" I said.

"No," she said. "I want to finish my coffee and admire your droopy drawers. Then I want to get in bed."

"I remember," I said sadly. "You don't want a cold, and I stay on the sofa."

"It's too late," she said, pulling a napkin from a cabinet and dabbing her nose, "I already caught your cold."

"Really," I grinned.

"Really," she grinned back, a kind of sad, friendly grin.

Ten minutes later we were in the small bed, sneezing, laughing, exploring and coughing. It was love time in the pneumonia ward. Her body was small and perfect. Mine was hard and scarred and imperfect—an attraction of opposites.

"What happened to your nose?" she said, kissing it.

"It put up a gallant but losing fight three times too many."

"I like it."

"It's hard to breathe through it, especially when I have a cold."

"Are you always this romantic?"

"Only when I'm inspired by royalty."

An idea hit me, and I rolled over on top of her and we both tumbled off the bed. We bounced together against the wall and stayed that way till someone knocked at the door. She squeezed away from me and called, "Who is it?"

"Ray."

"Just a second."

She put on an oversize purple robe and rolled her sleeves up. The bottom of the robe trailed on the floor. She padded barefoot to the door, looking like a kid trying to play grownup. I rolled over and pulled on my shorts.

"Peters," beamed Ray Narducy, a cab driver *sans* protective muffler. His hack hat was pushed back on his head and his glasses had a film of steam over them.

"Hi kid," I said.

"Find anything?"

"A little," I answered. "Our friends in the Caddy caught up with me, and I'm trying to keep out of their way."

He walked comfortably to the refrigerator, opened it, and looked for something to eat while we talked.

Merle reached over his head, standing on tiptoe to pull down a box of cookies and hand it to him.

"Need any help?" he said.

"Maybe later," I told him, "but not while they might be able to link your cab with me."

We sat around eating cookies and sneezing, swapping stories about the good new days, listening to Narducy's imitations of Herbert Marshall and Lum Abner. Merle yawned. I said I was tired. Narducy ate cookies and drank a quart of milk. Merle went to bed, and I told Narducy I had to get up early. He said he did too and stayed twenty minutes more, giving me the plot of the last episode of "Lights Out."

When he left, I flew back into the bed with a grunt and a wheeze.

"Asleep?" I whispered.

"No," she said. She leaned over in the dark and kissed me. "But I've had enough action for the night, on top of a fever. Let's sleep on our memories."

I dreamed something, but I don't know what. When I woke up in the early morning light I held it in the palm of my memory, but it flittered away on dusty moth wings. Merle was still asleep, snoring through a congested nose. The room was full of romance and germs. I got dressed, shaved in the kitchen sink to be quiet, and left a note saying I'd contact her that night. Then I went out in the snow to find a phone. I found one at a lunch counter, where I ate Choco-nuts cereal and had two cups of coffee. It was about nine on Sunday morning, and the place was empty except for me and a guy with a kid he kept patting on the head everytime the kid said anything. Since the kid was only about two, he had a lot to say, but not much of it was clear. I listened for a while and watched. Something like nostalgia or longing started to get to me. I knew I'd have to pull away, or go through some somber hours envying that man with the kid.

Kleinhans wasn't at the Maxwell Street Station, but he had left a message for me to call him at home. They gave me his home number, and I heard the now familiar, but fuzzy voiced Sergeant Chuck Kleinhans.

"What time is it?"

"After nine," I said. "What have you got for me?"

"A large , heavy chair given to me by my grandfather when he came to this country. There's still enough strength in these old arms of mine to lift it above my head and bring it down on yours."

"I've offended you," I said sadly.

He tried to hold back a laugh.

"I'd say you have Peters, and you can ill afford to lose what little patience I have left. When we were in the State Street station a few hundred years ago, you called Indianapolis."

"Is that a question or a statement?" I said, looking back at the dad and kid who were cutting each other's waffles.

"It is a warning. Besides owing the City of Chicago a dollar and sixty cents, you played me for a sap."

"I'm sorry," I said. "I couldn't resist it. Cops bring out the trickster in me."

His yawn was enormous.

"I checked on the Canetta kid. He has a Chicago record three sheets long."

"You have an address for him?"

"Yeah," said Kleinhans with a sigh, "and not that old Ainslie junk the Indiana cops had. He's on probation and living at 4038 West Nineteenth Street. You wanna check him, go ahead. I don't think he's connected."

"What about my little old man?"

"Forget it. You didn't give me enough to frame a nigger newsman."

"How about a sheeny grocer?"

"Yeah," chortled Kleinhans, exhausting his range of over-the-phone emotions, "know one?"

"My old man. Stay in touch, Kraut."

I hung up, knowing Kleinhans would forgive and forget, or hold it against me for turning his words against him. If he was a normal respectable human being, he'd remember.

The snow was an inch thick outside. I looked into the grey sky and into the coffee shop window at the father-son team. The kid had spilled chocolate milk, and the father was cleaning it up with a proud smile. I felt like shit and wondered why I had missed Christmas.

My cash supply was down, and I didn't have time to call Louis B. or Warren Hoff. There was also a chance that if I did, they'd tell me I was fired. That wouldn't stop me from what I was doing, but it would cut into my fraying pocket. As long as they didn't fire me, they owed me for each day I worked.

I got on a streetcar, where a thin conductor with gloves and a blue uniform gave me a transfer and told me to go to the Loop and take a Douglas Park train to Pulaski Road. The ride to the Loop was short, and the straw mat seats of the streetcar cold, but I kept my mind off Chicago's environment by making entries in my little book of expenses. The book was growing thick with breakfasts, cabs, phone calls, cold tablets, hotel bills, Kleenex, gambling losses, and top coats.

Downtown, I climbed the steps to the El trains at State and Lake and waited for a Douglas Park train. The wait was long and cold. Trains didn't run very often on Sunday. A Negro woman waited with me and some loud teenage kids with big city bluster. The kids were about thirteen, too old to be cute and too young to smash in the mouth. I tried to get past the fear of pneumonia by remembering the small, soft body and warm mouth of Merle G. It helped.

When the one-car train pulled in, the loud kids pushed ahead and ran to the front. The old woman moved to the back and so did I. There weren't many people on the train, and the car was cold and noisy as it rattled and teetered around the Loop and headed west on tracks thirty feet above the ground. Out the window on my side I couldn't see the tracks, just the street below and the houses a few feet away. A nagging worry about the body of Leonard Bistolfi and the possible reasons why he was killed in my hotel room intruded on my fear of falling to my death. Each turn gave me a shiver of panic, and I had to tell myself that these trains had been running in Chicago for more than forty years. My old man had mentioned them once when I was a kid, after he had visited his sister in the Windy City.

Neighborhoods shot by outside the iced window. Churches, old and heavy. Wind went wild down narrow streets, lifting sheets of snow in jerky dances. I shivered through a few dozen stops at wooden platforms. A family got on at someplace called Ashland, sat in front of me, and overlapped around me. The parents—dark, pale and serious—spoke in a European language that wasn't German, French, Spanish, or anything like them. It was deep and slushy, a language spoken in the back of the mouth and deep in the throat, a language to keep the cold out—Russian or Polish maybe. Three dark, pale kids, two boys, one girl, pushed their noses to the cold windows and chattered in their language and in English. Every once in a while one of them moved near their talking parents, who would touch the child's face or hair absently and lovingly.

It made me try to remember how my brother's two kids looked—David and Nate. I couldn't remember, probably because I hardly ever went to see them. I decided to bring them a present from Chicago when I went back home, but I didn't know what a Chicago present might be.

The conductor called out "Crawford Avenue, Pulaski Road," and I got out with the happy family and went down a flight of rusty metal steps to the street. At a newsstand outside the station door, a chunky old man shifted from foot in front of a metal garbage can with a fire going inside it. The Sunday Chicago papers were fat, and I couldn't carry one, so I just asked him which way Nineteenth Street was. He told me to head north two blocks and there I'd be. I hustled through the snow past a storefront hot dog place named Vic's, with a cartoon of a guy eating a sandwich on the window. The steamy smell of red hots and onions came through the closed door. I thought of stopping by, but went on past a closed candy store, a cleaning store, a Polish meat market with a sign in the window for blood soup, and a corner tavern called Mac's.

One place was open on the street—a gas station

where a skinny, serious-looking kid wearing a baseball cap and earmuffs was changing a tire. I crossed the street and walked over to him. He paused every few seconds to blow on his cold red fingers.

"Forty thirty-eight Nineteenth," I said.

He pointed down the street behind the gas station.

"Know a kid named Canetta?" I tried. "Wears an orange jacket?"

He nodded that he knew him.

"What do you know about him?" I said, plunging my hands deep in my pockets and shifting like the newsy from leg to led.

"Enough not to talk about him to people I don't know," said the kid in a surprisingly deep voice as he pulled the tire free from the jacked-up DeSoto.

"I'm not a friend," I said.

The kid sort of smiled.

"He's lived around here maybe two months. Brought a car in once with Indiana plates. Goes out of town a lot."

"Ever see him with anyone?"

The kid lifted a fixed tire and heaved it onto the wheel.

"Yeah," he said with a grunt as he adjusted the tire. "Kind of big guy was in the car yesterday. Had a hat on, didn't get out or talk. They just got gas. Nothing else I can give you."

He tightened the lugs on the wheel, stood up, and warmed his hands under his arms before dropping the car.

"Thanks a lot," I said. "Aren't you going to ask why I want to know?"

He shook his head no.

"If I don't ask, I don't know when someone else asks. Makes it easier."

"You got a point," I said and headed down Nineteenth.

There was an empty lot on the corner of Nineteenth and Komensky. Some kids wearing thin jackets were playing football in the snow. They called each other Al, Irwin, and Melvin and they screamed and laughed. One of the kids had one arm.

Forty thirty-eight was a three-story yellow building across from a wide, three-block long prairie. Cars were parked in the prairie near the street. The wind ran over a field of frozen weeds, hitting the cars and rocking them. The ground around the cars was covered with tire ruts made in the rain and now frozen solid and partly filled with shifting snow. A little kid sat in the recess of a narrow window on one side of the entrance to the building. The recess kept the worst of the wind away. The kid was about six, with a knit green cap over his head and ears. He wore corduroy knickers and a fuzzy jacket too light for the weather. The kid watched the cars and wind and played with a loose tooth in the front of his mouth.

"Hi," I said pulling my collar around my neck. "My name's Toby Peters. I'm a detective. What's your name?"

"Stgsmmm," he said, with a finger in his mouth.

"Stugum?"

"No," he said with weary patience removing his finger, "Stu-ard."

"You live here?"

"Yuh."

"Know a guy named Canetta? Wears an orange jacket?"

A sour look crossed Stu-ard's face. His head went up and down once, showing he knew him.

"Second floor. Over us."

"He there now?"

"Yuh, another guy too. Maybe two other guys."

"You know the guys?"

"One's Morris, comes here sometimes. I don't know the other guy—a big guy I seen here yesterday."

"Thanks," I said, opening the door. "What are you doing out here in the cold?"

"Hit my baby sister and ran away," he said, going back to his tooth. I gave him my scarf and wrapped it around his neck awkwardly, getting a suspicious look.

"Detectives get scarves free," I explained

"Detectives catch rats?" he said.

"Yeah," I said. "Dirty rats and killers."

"I mean real rats," the kid explained. I thought I saw a drop of blood on his gum from the squirming tooth. "We caught one in the phoney fireplace today. My dad's home."

I went inside and found Canetta's name on the mailbox, scrawled in pencil right on the metal. The downstairs door in the hall was open. The hall was clean. I went up squeaky steps covered with clean but tired carpeting and stopped in front of the two doors on the second floor.

Behind the door on the left I could hear the bark of a small dog, and a woman shouting, "Quiet, Peanuts." Then she said something like, "Sheldon will find out about the noise when he gets home."

I decided that wasn't my door. The wind sang bass as I tried the handle on the second door and held my other hand on the .38, which lay cool and comfortable in my coat pocket.

The door was locked. I decided to knock and heard something scuttling inside—maybe one of the rats the kid downstairs had mentioned. Maybe one of the rats I was looking for. My nose was running again, but I didn't have time or a free hand. I knocked again and thought I heard the scuttling sound move toward the door. It came slow and as it got closer, it sounded more like the dragging foot of the mummy from some Universal picture.

"Hello," I said with a heavy Yiddish accent picked up from vague memories of my grandfather, "is here a Mister Canetta? I'm from landlord mitten da pipes."

Someone fumbled at the lock inside and I stepped back, expecting to face the kid who had tried to steal my suitcase and whose nose I had broken. The door came open a crack and stayed that way.

"Somevone dere?" I asked. No answer.

I took a deep breath, wiped my nose on my sleeve, pulled out the gun and pushed the door open. I jumped inside and was about to go flat on the floor when I saw him. He was about three or four feet from me in a little reception area. His back was against a mirror on the outside of a closet. His knees were slightly buckled and his mouth was open. Blood trickled from his mouth and poured from his belly. He was a good thirty years older than Canetta—a little guy with a balding head gasping for air he couldn't get. I moved to him, keeping low in the dark apartment. There was a living room behind me with some light coming in from the morning, but it wasn't much of a morning.

The living room was furnished with dark, heavy furniture. I kept my back to it, and my eyes down the dark hall going the other way. With my free arm I helped the man sag to the floor. I had never seen him before, but I had the feeling he might be the Chico double I was looking for. The age and size were right. The face and features were probably close, but it was hard to tell. The face in front of me was twisted in pain and surprise. No one would mistake him for a Marx Brother if he were in the same room with the Brothers, but a good bluff might carry it off.

He tried to say something, and his eyes moved in the direction of the hall. I nodded to him that I understood, but I didn't understand a goddam thing. Something gurgled inside of him and moved up his chest to his throat. It rattled his body and killed him. I lowered him gently and looked at myself in the bloody mirror. My hands were shaking. I held my breath for the count of ten and stepped as quietly as I could over the body and toward the apartment's hall. The floor was uncarpeted and made of boards that squeaked above the outside wind like a carpenter driving nails.

I moved along the wall, my back against it and my gun pointing forward. A blast of machine gun fire would cut through me like the man in the alcove before I could get off a shot. I hoped the guy with the chopper was gone, but I couldn't be far behind him. My feet slipped slightly in something wet and sticky, probably the trail of blood from the dead guy who had let me in.

I hit an open door and put as little of myself into it as I could. It was a bedroom with a single window, a single chest of drawers, a painting of a peacock on the wall, and a closet with holes in it. The holes made a curving line, as if someone had done a graph of the weather or stock market in bullets. The man in the hall had probably been shot in the closet, I thought, but something changed my mind—a sound from the closet. I inched along the wall and kicked the door open. There was nothing at eye level and only a few shirts on the hangers inside. Sitting on the floor with a pair of pants and a wire hanger in his clenched fingers was the kid who had tried for my suitcase in Indianapolis. I couldn't see much of him in the dark, but I saw enough. His nose was bandaged where I had hit him, but it would take more than bandages to take care of what had happened to him now.

One of the bullets that went through the closet had hit him in the neck. Another two had caught him high on the chest. He wasn't as messy as the guy in the other room, but it looked just as fatal. He saw me and tried to say something.

I got low and moved into the closet, keeping my eyes jumping from him to the bedroom door.

"Get cop," he sputtered, and started to cough.

"I'll call the cops," I said. "They'll be here in a few minutes. Who shot you?"

He looked at me as if I were crazy. His eyes open wide and his head moved back and forth. He wet his lips to say something, opened his mouth wide, let out a guttural sound and froze, looking at me. It was a still photograph, a frozen frame of film and time. He would look at me forever unless I moved, because he was dead.

But I didn't move. The closet door did. It slammed with a crack. I froze.

The question was: was there something about me that made people want to use me for a bullet pin cushion? Did I ask for it by looking like a victim or a person who was worth a quarter of a pound of lead, but not a quarter of an hour of conversation? Those are the kinds of things you think of when you expect to have someone fill you full of holes. At least that's what I thought. The experience is free for those who have a chance to test it and survive.

Maybe, I thought, I like having people shoot at me. That made me think of my brother's bullet hole, the only one he had. He didn't get his on the street chasing some stupid kid who robbed a candy store. He didn't get his from a former movie star who thought he was coming too close to a secret. He didn't get his from a mob triggerman in a closet. Phil Pevsner got his in the great war.

Phil had enlisted in 1917 when he was twenty-two. He was big and tough and angry at the Germans. Then he caught a long, thin pointed German rifle bullet in his stomach in some Belgian woods, during some battle that didn't make the newspapers and was a cinch to miss the history books. Phil had a medal to show for it. The medal had been worth two bucks and a job as a cop. I was sure Phil now imagined suspects as German soldiers—the German soldiers he never got his hands on.

In honor of Phil's failure to get to the Germans

during the war, I had renamed our old dog Murphy, Kaiser Wilhelm, knowing Phil's fondness for throwing a kick at the animal if I wasn't around. Phil never really appreciated my consideration. Someplace I had a photograph of Phil just before he shipped out for the week he would spend in Europe. He had his uniform pants tucked into shiny boots, his neat jacket, and his doughboy cap right on the top of his head with the chin strap tight under his chin.

Nostalgia was getting me nowhere. With a corpse in my lap, and my back against a cold wall, I started to feel a chill. I could do without irony. I had found the flu in Chicago, but had avoided the backache I had almost learned to live with. If my back hit now, the triggerman wouldn't even have to shoot. He could just leave me sitting against the cold wall in a cramped position for an hour or two, and I'd never be able to stand up straight again.

Maybe, I thought, I could yell through the door and persuade the killer that I was the harmless remnant of a man, a soon to be elbow-shaped creature worthy of curiosity, not hatred or fear. Those were my semidelirious thoughts at the top level of consciousness. I shared them with the still warm corpse of a kid named Bitter Canetta, who had plenty to be bitter about.

Someplace a lot deeper down, I knew I was going to get on my knees and hope my back had enough spring left in it for me to get out of the closet fast, and possibly hit the killer before he could hit me.

I listened for footsteps, but I couldn't tell. The wind and creaking of the building didn't help at all, and the rats scurrying in the walls weren't cooperating.

There was a thin space between the bottom of the closet door and the floor. The morbid winter grey light spread through the bullet holes and under the door, but not very far. Clouds and daydreams of killers darkened the beams.

My back tightened low on the left but let me get up on my knees. I had to lift Canetta off of me and into the corner, but there wasn't much room for moving and lifting in the closet. I remembered seeing something with Lillian Gish years before in which Donald Crisp had locked her in a dark closet. She went crackers, thrashing all over, screaming. I wondered if Al Capone had felt like Lillian Gish when he was on Alcatraz. I wondered if he had felt the way I did in that closet.

My foot slipped on a shoe and some old newspaper. My agility and silence made the USC marching band sound like silent prayer. I was sure I heard something outside the door, in the bedroom. I was sure I saw a shadow through the holes in the door. My knees ached, but my back felt all right. I thought of putting my eye next to one of the bullet holes in the door, but the thought of getting shot in the face made me sick to my stomach. I'd seen a few with slugs in the face. I backed as far as I could against the wall with my gun in my hand, reached out for the handle, and shot my 160 pounds out of the door. The door banged open behind me, closed and open again.

My spring sent me forward toward where I figured the gunman was, but he wasn't. I hit the bed and flew over it against the window. The window quivered and held. As I slid to the floor, losing my gun, I got a glimpse of the concrete courtyard two flights down. I could have been splattered on it if I had gone through the glass.

If anyone had been in the room I would have been dead, if he weren't convulsed with laughter. It would take a pretty wild joker to find the whole thing funny, but my pal with the chopper didn't seem to be too upset by the corpses he was leaving. I scrambled for my gun, making more noise, and having the flash of an idea that the killer might want to be found and was leaving corpses as Hansel and Gretel left pieces of bread or ginger ale or whatever. If I survived, and he killed enough people, I might be able to follow the trail to him. I also remembered that for some reason Hansel and Gretel's trick didn't work and that I hadn't believed in fairy tales for thirty-five years.

I finally got both hands on my .38 and got up with it. The dead Canetta just looked at me dumbfounded. It was winter in a freezing apartment, and I was sweating.

I wanted to inch my way back to the front door as fast as I could and get the hell out of there. I wanted to tell myself that I had arrived too late and the killer was long gone. But I knew it couldn't be so. With the bullet holes in them, Canetta and the other guy hadn't been a long time dying, and besides, the kid downstairs had said three men were up here. I sat listening, trying to hold my breath. I thought I heard a squeak of floor somewhere in the back of the apartment, further into the darkness of that hall. It didn't have to be a person. It didn't have to be someone waiting me out, but it probably was.

I got off the squeaking bed, knowing that if someone was back there he sure as hell knew that I was there and had found his bodies. I could have opened the window and yelled "help" into the wind, but I went back to the hall.

A shot lit up the darkness like a flaired match and whistled past my head down the hall. It wasn't a machine gun. I jumped back into the bedroom and heard fast footsteps and the opening of a door.

I went back into the hall, took a shot down the hall to lead the way, and went carefully but fast in the direction of the door sound. I found a toilet and a small dining room that led into a smaller kitchen with a worn yellowish linoleum floor. The back door was open, and the storm door banged in the wind.

I stepped out onto the grey painted wooden porch and listened. I could hear clotheslines creaking and footsteps hurrying below me. I leaned over the railing into the whirling snow and looked down at an empty concrete courtyard. A figure wearing a dark coat and carrying a black case ran across the open space toward the corner of the building. I leveled my pistol and took a shot. Chips of brick sprayed near his head. He didn't look back.

I ran down the steps, slipping a couple of times on the patches of ice. Somewhere I could hear the wail of police sirens over the weather and the thubbing of my heart. Someone, maybe the old lady who was waiting for Sheldon, had called the cops about machine-gun shots. Even with the wind, someone must have heard what looked like at least forty rounds of explosion.

Running across the snowy sidewalk of the court-yard, I turned the corner and ran through a passageway to a street. Half a block ahead I could see the figure with the suitcase. I figured I had been lucky. I had arrived when he had put the machine gun away. Whoever he was, even if he had a car waiting, couldn't carry a machine gun through the streets. That was why he had taken the shot at me with a hand gun. The few seconds I had stopped to talk to the kid downstairs had probably kept him from decorating the apartment with me along with Canetta and the little man.

I couldn't get a good look at the guy, who was moving pretty well on the empty streets in the snow considering the fact that he was carrying a fifteen pound machine gun in a suitcase.

Running was hard. No one shoveled the walks in this neighborhood. It was tough to cut the distance between us. Everytime I tried to hurry, I slipped, but I kept the distance between us the same. There were definitely police cars somewhere behind, but I didn't stop to worry about them. If the guy with the chopper had someone in a car waiting, it was far from where he had used his gun. If he had a car parked, I had stayed close enough to him to keep him from jumping into it without risking a clean shot from me as he took time to start it and drive away, especially on a snowy street.

We kept chugging through snow, my pants legs dripping wet, steam coming from my mouth. I didn't know what kind of shape he was in for a cross-country race.

He turned a corner and headed east toward Pulaski. I kept up. In two short blocks he crossed Pulaski. I had cut the distance by about fifteen feet and was sure I'd have him. He was slowing down. Then he got lucky. Streetcars didn't run often on Sunday in Chicago, but one pulled up at the corner as he crossed the street. It was heading north and he got on. I was too far away to catch it, and bothered by the blowing wind and low visibility to make out his face even if he had turned it toward me, which he carefully did not.

The red streetcar headed north and I stood panting. I still had some run left in me, but I wasn't sure I wanted to take on a streetcar. I decided to give it a try anyway. Maybe a cab would come by and I could catch it and the streetcar. There weren't many people on the street, which looked like it was normally commercial. Sunday and bad weather kept the number down to a handful as I trotted into unknown territory after the slow-moving streetcar.

It stopped to pick up a passenger on Sixteenth Street but pulled away before I could cut the distance very much. The sidewalks of Pulaski were shoveled reasonably clean, and I would have caught up with the streetcar on a day when it made normal stops to let off and pick up people. As it was, even with traffic lights, I kept it in sight. The streets moved up in numbers. By Twelfth Street, I had managed to keep from losing ground and I was sure the man with suitcase had not gotten off. But it was man against machine. The man was sucking in chilled air fast and feeling the pain of unfamiliar cold.

I leaned against a delicatessen on the corner of Twelfth and Pulaski and was stared at by a small, bearded man dressed entirely in black. He picked up a discarded cigarette butt that had melted a hole in a bank of shoveled snow and turned his back on me.

The streetcar and the killer had won. It pulled further into the blowing snow. I stood catching my breath, or trying to. When I could talk, I asked the bearded man where I could get a cab. He answered me in Yiddish. I said thanks and looked around for a cab. There wasn't any. I gave up and went into the delicatessen, sweating and panting.

At a booth away from the door, I put my hands on the warm table, waiting for the pain and trembling to pass. The place was full of families and couples having their Sunday meal out. The place was clean and plain, with the smell of hot food and onions.

"What'll it be?" asked a guy with a pot belly, a sour look, wild grey hair, and a white apron.

"A buck and a half of lunch, a friendly smile, and coffee."

His thick face moved into a bilious fake grin, and I let out a laugh—more of a laugh than the moment deserved, but I needed it. I was alive. The waiter shrugged, people looked at me and I tried to control myself.

The food was great—hot Jewish food, memories of childhood and a mother long gone. Chicago, murder, and disease had begun to turn me nostalgic. I ate the chopper liver, cold beet borscht with sour cream, kishke, boiled chicken, and rice pudding; downed my coffee, ate a piece of halvah, left a big tip, and asked the waiter how to get downtown. He told me and pocketed the tip without a comment.

I made it back to Merle's place by late afternoon. She was reading the Sunday paper and listening to Henry Aldrich on the radio. She made some coffee, helped me undress and made me warm all over. I told her my tale, enjoyed her hands on me and giggled once.

Then I fell asleep.

When I woke up, my watch told me it was night, and my eyes told me that Merle was still in her robe. She got dressed, told me what there was to eat, and said she was going out.

"I'm going to see my kid," she explained somewhat defiantly.

"I didn't ask," I said.

She smiled sadly and went out.

The phone was down the hall. I called Kleinhans' home number, figuring it was still Sunday, but he wasn't there. I tried the Maxwell Street Station number. He was there.

"Peters," he sighed enormously, a man of broad telephonic gestures. "What the hell happened on the West Side?"

"I went to see Canetta, but somebody was just ahead of me."

"We know all about your visit," he said. "Homicide wants to talk to you."

"They want to do more than talk, don't they?"

"Maybe so," he said. "I told them I thought you were clean. That I knew you were going to see Canetta, that you have no way of getting your hands on a chopper, but they want to talk. They've already got witnesses to your being there—some kid—and other witnesses saying you were in the neighborhood running around."

"Shit, Kleinhans," I said wearily, "you don't think I did it. You—"

"I don't think I like you, Peters, but I don't think

you did this either. You have to admit, three guys have been chopped down around you since you hit town less than two days ago, and you came here straight from a visit with Capone in Miami. I think you'd better come in and do some explaining."

"That'd keep me tied up too long," I said. "I'm still trying to save Chico Marx, remember?"

"Suit yourself," he said. "But the word's out for you and they've called for pictures of you from L.A. You don't come in, it's going to look bad and take you longer to get out and on your way back to L.A."

"Kleinhans, did you see the bodies from that place?"

"Yeah. One of them fits what you were saying about Marx having an impersonator, but the guy isn't that close. His name's Morris Kelakowsky, a harmless neighborhood guy who used to act in the Yiddish theater on Ogden Avenue. Did a little neighborhood gambling, small time stuff."

"He fits, doesn't he?"

"Yeah," Kleinhans admitted. "But I don't know what you're going to do with it now."

"Someone's knocking off everyone who might know about this gambling scam," I explained. "There's something to find out, and I keep getting close without knowing what I'm close to. Can you give me some time? How about your boss, the one who assigned you to watch me?"

There was a long beat before he answered.

"Sorry kid," he said. "We just don't have clout when there's a homicide. I'll back you if you come in."

"By the time I get out, Chico Marx could be

plowed under. Thanks anyway."

"Your funeral," he said. "I'll tell the homicide boys you called and what you said. It might keep them from blowing you up on sight."

I hung up and went back to Merle's room. I had chills and a lot to worry about. Nitti's gang and the cops were looking for me. My flu was worse. I still had Chico Marx to protect, and now a killer to catch.

I sweated into delirium on the bed, soaking it through, and got up around midnight with an idea. Merle had come back without my knowing it and had been placing cold washcloths on my head.

"Know why you let me in?" I said to her. "You're a mother cat. I'll bet you take in stray animals and feed them and find them homes."

Her smile said yes.

The sun came up, promising nothing—a small orange ball bouncing over the frigid mist of Lake Michigan. It wasn't the same sun I had seen in Miami. This was a puny younger brother who had no heat, only a useless smile. From the window in the Drake, I watched a small boat, probably a coast guard launch, heading slowly into the low steam. I listened to its motor gasp in brittle chugs over the water.

Chico and Harpo were playing gin rummy, smacking the cardboard rectangles on the table. Chico beamed through the game, uttering *uhs* and delighted *ahs* while we waited for a phone call.

Groucho lay on the bed reading the newspaper. He looked at me and shook his head.

"We're an anachronism, a relic of the past, a clown

for people who've never been to the circus, a dialect comic for people who don't remember vaudeville, a fast-talking, baggy-pants comic with a leer for those who were afraid to go to burlesque. We're a trio of dinosaurs, an endangered species lying around a hotel in Chicago waiting for someone to come through the door and shoot us."

"No one's going to shoot you, Grouch," Chico said, without looking up from his cards. "They're going to shoot me."

"That's consoling. If I'm lucky, and they don't miss, all I'll lose is my brother instead of my life. I may be tired of playing that character in our movies, but I'm not tired of playing." He raised his eyebrows suggestively.

"Call Arthur," Chico said. "It'll make you feel better."

Groucho turned to me.

"My son Arthur," he explained, "thinks he's a tennis player, but he doesn't have to watch himself play. That's what I should be doing, following my son around from sunny villa to sunny country club, watching girls from the veranda while I sip cool drinks and complain about the heat."

"Then why are you here?" I said.

"Because he's my brother," sighed Groucho, looking at Chico. "He never memorizes his lines. He misses shows because he's out gambling. He throws his money away, but he's my brother. I'm younger than he is but I'm like a father to him."

Chico's hand went up in a mock denial, but his eyes stayed on his cards.

"Don't be crazy."

"Crazy, eh," said Groucho, throwing the paper down and opening his eyes wide. "They said Caesar was mad and Hannibal was mad and surely Napoleon was the maddest of them all."

"Eduardo Cianelli in *Gunga Din*," I said.

"That's right," said Groucho, throwing me a cigar and glaring at Chico. "Now Ciannelli is a great Italian actor."

"He was supposed to be an Indian in *Gunga Din*." said Chico, "but he kept his Italian accent. I could have played an Indian with an Italian accent."

"That's a good idea," said Groucho. "Let's see if we can get you cast as Geronimo. I'll suggest it to Mayer."

The phone rang. Groucho answered in a fake Southern Negro dialect.

"Yessuh. Yessuh, he right here suh. He shohly is."

He handed me the phone.

"Peters," I said.

"Mitch O'Brien at the *Times*. You wanted someone from City Desk to call you?"

"Right," I said. "I'm a reporter from the *Toronto Star* and I want to get in touch with Ralph Capone—an interview. Have any idea how I might do it?"

"What's your first name, Peters?"

"Tobias," I said. "Why?"

"Who's the city editor on the *Star*?"

"Tavalario," I said instantly. "New man. Old friend."

O'Brien laughed at the other end.

"O.K. Peters. Is the *Star* a morning or evening paper?"

"Evening," I guessed.

"What are the deadlines?"

"Ten, two and four," I said quickly.

I didn't like his laugh.

"You don't work for the *Toronto Star*. You work for Doctor Pepper. You're the guy the cops are looking for. Shit, you could at least have changed your last name."

"I didn't think they'd get to the papers with me."

"I'm a police reporter," he said. "I read all about you on the blotter last night."

Groucho had gone back to his paper. Harpo held a card up high, hesitating to throw it. Chico looked at the card, leered, and nodded his head, daring Harpo to drop the card.

Harpo let out a gookie, the puff-cheeked, cross-eyed idiot face from his movies. I had never really related the little man playing cards with the wild-haired idiot on the screen. The look startled me. Chico burst out laughing and Groucho smiled.

"That's been sure fire since he was a kid," Groucho explained. "When in doubt, pull a Gookie. It always cracks Chico and Gummo."

"Peters, what the hell is going on there?" It was O'Brien's voice over the phone.

"I was thinking," I said. "You win. Why are you talking to me?"

"Maybe a story," O'Brien said. I could hear the sound of voices behind him, somebody yelling, typewriters clacking.

"I checked you out with a couple of calls to L.A. I'm going to have a hell of a time explaining the expense if I don't come up with something. My source says you're straight—well, maybe a little bent—but you're not likely to start a machine gun spree."

"You never know," I said.

"I really don't give a shit," said O'Brien. "I'll give you a Capone phone number if you give me the story."

"Some things I can't talk about," I said, looking at the Marx Brothers. "I've got a client. I'll tell you what I will give you—a first person account about how I found the bodies."

"Is it bloody?" said O'Brien.

"Yeah," I said. "You'll love it."

"O.K., Peters, but I tell you in advance, it'll be fugitive gives his version of gangland style murders in exclusive interview with the *Times*."

"What the hell," I sighed. Then I told him about finding Bistolfi in the LaSalle and Canetta and Morris Kelakowsky in the West Side apartment. When I looked up, Harpo and Chico had stopped their game and were staring at me. Groucho's eyes had become narrow and serious.

"O.K.," said O'Brien. "It's good." He gave me a number, Independence 1349, and told me to call again if I had anything to trade.

I hung up. Six Marx eyes were on me as I got the desk and asked the operator to get me the number O'Brien had told me. In a few seconds it was ringing.

"Yeah?" said a voice.

"My name's Peters," I said. "Al Capone said I should look up his brother Ralph."

"Who're you?" The voice was that of a man who took his time, and yours, absorbing information. I told him who I was and repeated that Al Capone had told me to call. Then there was silence.

"Hello," a male voice said. This second voice was high but raspy, as if someone had cut it in two and pasted it back together, but did a bad job.

I repeated my tale about Al Capone, even mentioned Giuseppe Verdi, and asked if the guy on the other end was Ralph.

"What you want?" he replied.

"Nitti's men are after me. The cops are after me. I'm trying to save my client, Chico Marx, from getting cut down for a debt he doesn't owe, and Nitti won't listen."

The voice told me to keep talking, so I did.

"I need to get Marx and a guy named Gino Servi together to prove Marx isn't the guy who owes him. Nitti's going to have to stop trying to kill me and Marx long enough to listen."

"I think Chico Marx is funny," said the voice soberly.

I put my hand over the receiver and told Chico the guy at the other end thought he was funny. He shrugged his shoulders.

"I like the one doesn't talk, too," he said. "The other one talks too fast."

"Nitti doesn't think Chico's funny," I said.

"He has a right," said the voice reasonably. "I'll see what I can do about Nitti. I can't do anything about the cops. There was a time a few years back when I could. Understand?"

I said I did.

"I give you no promise," said the raspy voice. "Nitti might say no. And I'm going to check you out with Al. If he didn't give you the O.K., I'll be looking for you. You're Peters, right?"

"Right, And you're Capone, right?"

"Where do we reach you?" he said, avoiding an answer.

I suggested that I call back, but he wasn't having any.

"Page a Mr. Pevsner in the lobby of the Drake," I said. "I'll have someone answer it and get the message to me."

"Right," he said and hung up.

"That was very nice," said Groucho. "Very tricky. Who's going to pick up the message?"

"I will," I said. "There's no problem."

I proved there was no problem by looking at my watch and leaning back in my chair with a false yawn. There was a very good chance that Al Capone wouldn't remember who the hell I was, and the only other guy who could confirm the Miami meeting was Bistolfi, who had been permanently punctuated at the LaSalle. The chances were good to even that Capone or Nitti's men would soon be in that lobby ready to break the arm of whoever picked up their message, and would keep breaking it into smaller pieces till they were led to me. I figured I'd save them the trouble, and one of the Marxes a broken arm. The odds were bad if you were betting your life, but I had the feeling Chico, with his lousy gambling instinct, would have thought they were reasonable.

"Well," sighed Groucho. "I'm going upstairs to sit in on a regional convention here—the American Psychiatrist's Association."

"You got the right," said Chico, examining his cards and rubbing his chin pensively. "You played a horse doctor."

Groucho stood up, put on his jacket, combed back his hair, and tightened his mouth into a serious and pained grimace. He looked like a bored doctor.

"It's about time someone spoke up about Freud and his disciples," he said, moving to the door. His brothers ignored him, and Groucho went on. "I'm sick of that nonsense. 'Parents are responsible for all their children who turn out wrong. They hated their mother, father, or both. Show people had especially unhappy childhoods and made up for it by going into acting.' "

"I know," said Chico, still not looking up, but knowing what was coming. "You loved our mother and father."

"Our parents were wonderful people," Groucho went on. Harpo nodded in agreement and played a card, which Chico snapped up with a *ha-ha*.

"Our parents were terrific," said Groucho. "We had great times. We didn't go into show business to escape our home. We went into show business because my mother's brother was Al Shean, who was pulling down $250 a week. We wanted a piece of that."

"Analysis may have done some good for a handful of people," Groucho said, "but if I know, it left a lot of people with a hell of a lot less money. Well, maybe Doctor Hackenbush can get in a few words of scorn on the twelfth floor. Take care of yourself, Peters."

He exited and I went to the door.

"Toby," said Chico, without looking up, "you don't have to get yourself killed for me. Grouch just left the room because he was embarrassed to tell you that he and Harpo agreed to pay the $120,000 even if I don't owe it."

Harpo didn't look up from his cards.

"You want them to pay?" I said.

"Hell no," he said with a smile.

I left the room, closing the door behind me, and took the elevator down to wait for a message from the man with the raspy voice I assumed was Ralph Capone.

The lobby was crowded with men in dark suits and white name tags, pipes, and a few beards. I took a seat facing the door after buying a *Life* magazine for a dime. I flipped through it.

Some New Zealand soldiers in Libya were on the cover. There were stories about Nazis killing Poles, and the British effort to keep smiling through the bombs. There were two pages of pictures of a yogi doing contortions, and a piece on a newsy named Angie S. Rossitto, a thirty-five inch high midget who was running for Mayor of Los Angeles. "As short as I am," *Life* quoted him, "I won't sell the people short."

Somewhere around eleven in the morning, about thirty minutes after I had sunk into *Life* and the leather black chair, three familiar forms came through the front entrance. Costello's arm was still in a sling. Chaney was wearing a scarf. Maybe he had caught my cold, since I was pretty well rid of it. The juke box man came right after them. *Life* magazine covered my face, and I was nose-to-nose with a picture of Ingrid Bergman, but they knew I was around, or someone was who could lead them to me. The juke box stayed at the door while the other two moved forward with hands in pockets. It looked like Ralph Capone had turned me over to Nitti, but I didn't have time to be bitter. I got up slowly as two men passed by, talking close together and seriously. One of the men was fat. I moved behind him as they headed for the elevator.

Through the crowd, the two familiar figures bubbled in and out of sight, searching faces. I ducked, pretending to listen to the conversation of the two talkers. One guy was saying something about subconscious wishes.

If the elevator had come five seconds earlier, I would have made it clean—but you can check off the turning points of your whole life and punch them into total of a few minutes of chance and choices.

Chaney spotted me as the elevator doors were closing. I didn't think he'd take a shot at me in a crowded lobby, but I wasn't sure. I expected him to give out a yell or make a rush for me. Instead, his face twisted into a sour smile and he slowly moved forward.

The elevator filled and the doors closed before Chaney made it to a close-up. I thought fast: there were two or three of them coming for me. If they knew what they were doing, one would stay in the lobby, another would go up the staris, and the third would wait for the elevator and ask the operator if he remembered which floor I had gotten off. I had to figure they'd do it right. Nitti's boys weren't smart, but they had probably done things like this before.

One of the guys in front of me was smoking a cigar. He had a short grey beard and looked like a picture I had seen once of Sigmund Freud. I rode with Freud and his bunch up to twelve and followed them into a maroon-carpeted lobby. A desk with a white tablecloth and a sign over it reading "Registration" stood ten feet from the elevator. A smiling woman sat behind the desk, flanked by two unsmiling women. All three had flowers pinned over their right breasts. They looked like a plump, aging version of the Andrew Sisters getting ready to sing "You're a Lucky Fellow, Mr. Smith" to a roomful of recruits.

The woman in the middle looked at me hopefully and stood up. Her dress was a purple thing with big white flower patterns all over it. She nodded at me and I walked over, wondering if I should go to the fire escape. If they had the fire escape covered, that would be the worst way for me to go because there wouldn't be any witnesses out there. I considered calling the cops and hiding till they arrived, but that would be the end of protecting Chico. He'd have no choice but to accept his brother's offer. He was stubborn enough not to take that choice.

I walked to the registration table. It was covered with ash trays, dirty coffee cups, and a handful of unclaimed name tags.

"Yes," I said to the woman.

Her breath across the table was peppermint Life Savers.

"Registration, doctor," she said. "You are a bit late."

"Ah, yes," I smiled at her, glancing back at the elevator door. I picked up a name tag and the trio sighed in unison, as if an enormous burden had been taken from their backs.

"I'll just go tell Dr. Agabiti that you've arrived."

She hurried off in the crowd of coffee drinkers to find Dr. Agabiti, who would, on sight, expose me. I looked at my name tag. It read, "Dr. Charles Derry, Capetown, South Africa."

The peppermint lady bustled through the crowd with bobbing breasts and a tall, white-haired man held firmly against one of them. She nodded at me, and the tall man squinted through round, horn-rimmed glasses before he advanced on me with an extended right hand.

"Dr. Derry?" he asked, a bit surprised. I knew I didn't fit anyone's image of a doctor, but if I pulled it off, I might be able to get into one of the meeting rooms and hide till Nitti's crew had given us the search.

"Yes," I said, unsure of what a South African dialect should be. I started with a Germanic one and gave up quickly.

"I'm Tom Agabiti," he said holding my hand firmly in strong, thin, and very boney fingers. "We've been looking forward to your coming and had decided you weren't going to make it. The weather and everything. But you're here."

"I'm here," I agreed, looking around the lobby at the wallpaper and dark fixtures with an approving air. I clasped my hands behind my back and waited for him to leave me alone. He didn't, just stared at me with a silly grin.

"We've read your book with great interest," he said. "And we're all looking forward to hearing your thoughts. I don't mind telling you we didn't think we'd be able to get you away from your work for this conference. First time in the states, isn't it?"

"Yes," I said, continuing to look at the walls.

"Well," he sighed. "You made it, and right on time, too. Shall we go?"

"Of course," I said, trying to imitate the soft confidence of a psychiatrist I had once met.

Agabiti moved through the people in the lobby. There were a few women in suits, but it was mostly a male gathering. The crowd began to thin as we moved down the hall. People were going into little meeting rooms.

We went into a room through dark oak double doors. About fifty men and a couple of women were seated on folding chairs facing a table with a pitcher of water and two glasses. Many of them turned when Agabiti and I entered, and I looked for a seat. But Agabiti wasn't having any.

"No," he whispered. "You are on now."

He lead me to the little table, pointed to one of the two chairs, and put his hands together. It suddenly dawned on me, like the sun over Miami or the snow over Chicago, that I was to be the speaker, or rather the absent Dr. Derry was.

I decided to get the hell out of there, but my eye hit the door. Chaney put his head in and looked over the people seated. He didn't expect me to be at the head table. I sat down quickly and put my head in my hands as if I had a headache or was in the process of deep preparatory thought. Through my fingers, I saw Chaney go over the crowd and move back out of the room. He might come back. He might even ask the Andrew Sisters at the desk if they had seen someone with my description, a dark little guy about forty with a pushed-in nose. They'd sing out that I was Dr. Derry.

My best bet was to listen to what Agabiti was saying, but my mind kept exploring the thin blue stripes against the white of the wallpaper. Between the stripes, a recurrent pattern of designs that looked like old lanterns rose on top of each other. I was imprisoned by wallpaper and fifty faces looking at me and waiting.

"Dr. Derry," said Agabiti, "has not only studied with both Doctors Freud and Jung, but has been praised by both for his attempts to reconcile basic differences. As you know, his book *Super-Ego, and Ego vs. Self and Ego: A False Battle* is a pioneer work—a controversial work, but a work that promises to mend a schism, close a chasm." He showed his hands with outstretched fingers coming together slowly and firmly. "I could continue, but there would be little point when we have Dr. Derry here to speak for himself. He will speak briefly and then respond to questions. Dr. Derry."

They applauded and I smiled. The applause stopped and I poured myself a drink of water. There was something in the water. I showed Agabiti. He handed me the other glass. I inspected it to be sure it hadn't been used. Someone coughed. I poured water slowly and drank. Someone shifted and a chair creaked. I looked at my watch, the door, and the wallpaper, and stood up.

"My notes were lost on the plane from London," I said with a sad smile, indicating I would go on in spite of the burden, "so my comments will be brief. Super-Ego, Self and Ego," I said, looking at the faces in front of me and trying to do Paul Muni. "I think it is a false battle because we have not yet clearly defined what we mean by those terms."

There were a few nods of agreement, so I went on.

"I've studied with both Freud and Jung," I said humbly, wondering who the hell Jung might be, "and I tell you frankly I'm not sure that either of them has defined the terms to the point where it is reasonable to say a real battle exists."

More nods of approval, but even more nods of disagreement.

"I don't mean there isn't a real point of controversy," I said quickly, looking directly at one of the people who hadn't liked what I had said. "There's a difference between controversy and battle. What I am calling for and what I call for in my book is a concentration on definitions. Until we define, we are doing ourselves, our patients and patients for a hundred years to come a disservice."

Some wild applause.

"We are physicians first," I said holding up a finger, "and psychiatrists second."

They were talking among themselves, approving, nodding, arguing as I paused to take a long drink. Dr. Agabiti was grinning up at me with his arms crossed. I held up my hands.

"I've had a long, difficult trip," I said. "Time zones and all that. And I just arrived. So, I'll move right to the questions."

One of the two women in the room stood up, pursed her lips and said,

"I don't quarrel with your desire for definition, Dr.

Derry, but I fail to see how definitional problems are involved in the issue of Jung's acceptance of a collective unconscious and Freud's rejection of it."

I nodded sagely, looked at Dr. Agabiti as if we both knew the answer and spoke.

"You are absolutely right," I said. "It is a basic problem. It is something that cannot be reconciled and therefore it is something we accept and build on."

I punched my fist into my hand for emphasis, expecting someone to rise from the audience and throw a chair at me. No one did.

The next question came from a young man with a Boston accent. His hair was brown and wavy. In five years he'd be fat. I could see he didn't like Derry.

"Nothing you have said so far, Dr. Derry, has any substance," he said. "You've been evasive. What if I were to say that the case history in your book of Roy Wood's breakdown revealed clearly that your suggested approach is of no value in affecting a cure?"

"I would simply disagree," I said.

"And what if I were to say that your refusal to mention the drug used in that case indicates an unethical refusal to share medical knowledge that could help patients? Either your approach is without merit and insufficiently tested, or you should mention now before this body the specific drug you used."

The assembly thought this was a reasonable request. They had me. I could make up a drug, but they'd know it was a fake, or I could think up some real drug I had seen on Shelly Minck's shelf back in the dental office. If they believed me, some of the people in the room might try it, and I had no idea what Shelly's drugs might do to some poor nut.

"Well?" said Boston, his hands folded in front of him.

"The drug is scapalomine," said a voice in the back of the room. "Dr. Derry doesn't want to mention it because he and I are still conducting experiments in Capetown."

Groucho Marx stood up and continued. "I'm the chief of staff at Dr. Derry's hospital in Capetown, and I suggested that he not give the information, but under the circumstances and with the warning I've just given, I think it will do no harm now."

"Dr.—" Boston began.

"Hackenbush," said Marx seriously. I expected a roar of laughter or recognition, but there was none. Maybe the doctors never went to the movies. "And now, gentlemen, I'd like to talk to Dr. Derry in the hall for a moment. I know this is unprecedented, but if you'll just bear with us, I think I can persuade Dr. Derry to reveal something that will be of great scientific interest."

Agabiti looked confused and gazed around the room. No one appeared to know what to do.

"I don't think you can convince me, Dr. Hackenbush," I said somberly, "but I'll listen. I'll be right back."

I hurried quickly through the door with Marx and whispered to him as we got in the hall.

"Where did you get that scapolmine business?"

"It's true," said Groucho, "I read this quack Derry's book and asked some questions out at U.S.C.

The drug is probably scapalomine."

"You read medical books?"

"Of course," he said. "I'm a doctor, aren't I! Now what were you doing in there?"

I explained about Nitti's boys as we passed the Andrew Sisters, who looked surprised to see me out so early. There was no one else in the twelfth floor lobby. Everyone was in the various meeting rooms. In one room, there would be a long wait for Dr. Derry and Hackenbush to return.

"My advise as your physician," whispered Marx, "is to get the hell out of here. Let's get back to our room and shove you under the bed."

We pushed the button for the elevator, and Marx kept going through the pantomine of serious conversation. Our chances looked good. Nitti's men weren't in the lobby, and they had a lot of territory to cover. A few seconds later I drastically revised our chances. Costello was in the elevator. He stood back against the wall with his hand in his coat pocket. There was no running from him. I nodded toward Costello so Groucho would know, and we stepped in as the doors closed.

I wondered if Costello would shoot Marx, me, and the blissfully unaware elevator operator, or try to get me out where he could handle my demise slowly and painfully. I thought that painful demises were more his style.

He leaned over my shoulder with familiar garlic breath.

"I got a message," he whispered. "Tonight at eleven, you be at the New Michigan with Marx. Servi will be there. You got the message?"

"I got the message."

"Good," he said. "Things don't go right, I get you."

Groucho and I rode down with Costello to the lobby and watched him leave with the other two. He had probably thought Groucho was Chico.

"What was that all about?" asked Groucho as we got back in the elevator.

"My pal Al Capone remembered me," I said.

O.K., I told myself. Assuming Servi does get Chico off the hook, you still have two questions. First, who killed Bistolfi, Morris Kelakowsky, and Canetta? The second problem was tied to the first—how to get the Chicago cops to unlist me as public enemy number three or four and moving up fast. The most obvious solution to problem one was that at least four people were involved in some scheme to cheat the mob and Nitti out of $120,000. The killer was determined not to split that money into smaller chunks. Maybe Killer was worried about my getting too close. That led to an obvious conclusion. Killer might want me dead now unless there wasn't anyone left for me to get information from.

He might also realize, if he was a member of either

Nitti's or Capone's group, that as soon as Servi cleared Chico, Nitti might start looking for him.

That got me just about nowhere, so I decided to solve problem number two. I got directions and headed South on Michigan Avenue. The wind knocked over an old lady in a black coat. She didn't break her fall when the blast of iced air threw a block under her. The wind deserved a fifteen yard penalty for clipping. Instead, the old lady lost about three yards. She got up, determined. The first and ten looked like it might be the Old Water Tower I passed on Chicago Avenue. I never found out. The old lady was still half a block back, struggling against the blast. I was a foreigner and more determined. Chicago had thrown its best flu at me, and I had made it through almost five days. I adjusted my ear muffs and leaned my way down Michigan, past book shops and fancy women's stores with stiff-backed mannequins in their windows. In ten minutes, I made it past the *Tribune* Tower and across a bridge over the Chicago river. Ten minutes beyond that I was at City Hall on Clark. When I got to the one-block square lump, I kept my head down, pretending to fight the wind, but really keeping my face covered from the cops who were walking in and out.

I headed for the mayor's office, not that I expected to get in to the mayor, but because I needed information I could get there. A receptionist sat inside the door marked "Mayor". She looked young, red-haired and Irish. Her teeth were small and her smile long gone for the likes of me.

"Yes sir," she said.

"I'd like to see the mayor's secretary," I said.

"Do you have an appointment?" she said, looking past me for someone who was expected.

"No," I said, "but I have only one question and I'm a busy man." I looked at my watch. "If Chicago won't help me, Detroit will."

She was unimpressed, so I went on.

"I'm from Metro Goldwyn Mayer studio," I whispered. "We're thinking seriously of shooting a picture here next year about the Chicago Fire—a big thing, millions of dollars."

She was suspicious, but she couldn't afford to make the kind of mistake that might happen if she kicked me out.

"Did you see Mr.—"

"No," I said with a patient smile. "I saw no one. This is to remain strictly confidential until I get some reassurances from the Mayor's office directly."

She could have asked why I was telling her, but she didn't look that sharp. She wasn't.

"Let me check, Mr.—"

"Pevsner," I said. "Tobias Pevsner. If you'd like to call Mr. Mayer's office, I'll be glad to give you the number, Miss—"

"Kelly," she said with a small smile.

I had discovered from the directory in City Hall that the Mayor's name was Kelly, but I didn't think it was the moment to note the coincidence.

"Kelly," I mused. "A good name for a lovely young lady. You remind me very much of Vivien Leigh. Hey. Viv will be starring in the Chicago picture and she'll have a younger sister. Ever done any acting?"

Her mouth dropped and closed.

"A little, in a school play, *Arsenic and Old Lace*. I played the girl."

I pulled out my black expense book and gnawed pencil.

"Your first name?"

"Maureen, Maureen Kelly."

I wrote an expense item for a fifty cent breakfast and closed the book. She left and I looked around the bare little office with a single window facing nothing. It was a dreary place, and the man Maureen Kelly led out to see me fit perfectly. He was a prune of a man, pinched in by what must have been an enormous, tight rubber band under his jacket. Bowel movements must have been torture for him. His words fit the image— brief, clipped darts of words that traveled straight and allowed no echo.

"Yes," he said.

"Pevsner," I said, not bothering to extend my hand. My plan was to one-up him on bad manners and efficiency before he could get the chance. "I haven't much time so I'll be brief. I want to know if the City of Chicago will cooperate in the making of *A Song in the Fire*. If not, we'll shoot it on the lot and use Detroit for the exteriors."

"I see," said Prune, giving the evil eye to Maureen Kelly. "And what will this cost the city?"

"Cost?" I said, looking at him in disbelief. "Why should it cost? We're prepared, in fact, to make certain guarantees for housing, publicity, food contracts, local talent, security."

"I see," said Prune, trying to smile and failing. "Well, perhaps I can arrange a short meeting with the Mayor."

"Well," I said. "It's either now or not at all. I'm on a very tight schedule."

"Well, give me just a few minutes to check," he said. "I'll be right back."

"A few minutes is about all I can spare."

The prune went through a door marked "Private" and Maureen Kelly smiled at me—a pale smile from a child of the city made anemic in the molehill of City Hall.

"Can I get you anything?" she said. "Coffee?"

"Yes," I said. "Coffee."

She went through a second door, and I moved quickly to the one Prune had gone through. I could hear him talking inside, but I couldn't make out the words. I put one hand on the door and turned the handle slowly and gently till it was open a thin crack.

Prune's voice came through clearly.

"Late thirties or early forties, hair greying at the temples, about my height, with a flat nose. No I don't think he's dangerous, and I don't know how he got past Alex. No. Of course not. He's in the reception room of the Mayor's office. That's right. No, I do not know what you're waiting for. Get up here fast."

As he put down the phone I closed the door and turned to find Maureen with a steaming cup in the hand. My grin was enormous.

"Hold that for me just one second," I said. "I have to find the men's room."

I lowered my hands and moved leisurely but distinctly to the outer door, closing it behind me on the image of the slightly bewildered Maureen Kelly. There were a few people in the tile-floored hall. The sound of footsteps and the shaft of light from a single window make it feel like an old drugstore. I hurried to the stairway and went up half a flight. The footsteps from below were heavy and slower than they should have been. Leaning over the rail, I saw three blue uniformed cops come up and run down the hall toward the mayor's office with guns drawn, ready to blow away intruders and complainers.

I went down behind them with one hand on the rail, going two steps at a time. When I hit the main floor I lifted my collar, regretted giving my scarf to the kid on the West Side, and walked to the nearest exit. A cop stood in the street looking toward me. I retreated back into the cool echoes of the hallway. The cop from outside came through the door. In the few seconds it took for his eyes to adjust to the grey electric light, I opened the nearest door, went in and closed it behind me.

I was in a small office with two men. A thin guy in a white shirt with a big Adam's apple leaned over a guy at a desk who looked like a cop. The guy at the desk was short, stocky but not fat, with serious dark eyes. He was about my age, and wearing a neat, dark suit. His clothes reminded me of the uniforms Catholic kids had to wear in high school. His eyes met mine and I knew he was going over the description of the mad chopper killer. Instead of turning away and rushing into the possibility of a waiting cop outside the door, I smiled and stepped forward with my hand out.

"My name's Derry, Charles Derry," I said. "From

Cleveland—Maple Heights, really. Looking into some investment possibilities. Contacting politicians, people around City Hall."

The stocky man didn't get up and he didn't take my hand. Without taking his eyes from me he said to the thin man, "Thanks Ed." Ed looked at me suspiciously and backed away from the desk. The stocky man said nothing until Ed had left the room.

"Ed's a waiter at Henrici's around the corner, brings food over for people when they can't get away from the desk." He nodded to the desk in front of him and I notices a plate of food.

"The special," he explained. "Fried scallops, julienne potatoes, cole slaw, rolls and pie and coffee for seventy-five cents. Not as good as eating at home but the next best thing."

He opened his palm and pointed to a chair next to the desk. I sat down and watched him eat for about five minutes.

"My name's Daley, Richard Daley," he said, pushing a fruit cup toward me like a short college lineman giving a handoff. I took the fruitcup and a spoon. "I'm a state senator," he went on, "and I didn't shake your hand for a reason. You picked the wrong guy for a patsy, fella. So, eat your fruit cup and walk out of here."

He spoke with what seemed a careful choice of words, almost rehearsed, but delivered with an accent that said he would never get rid of the old neighborhood where guys said *duh* instead of *the* and *gunna* instead of *going* to or even *gonna*.

"Your name's not Derry," he said, sitting back warily with his hands on the desk while I ate the fruit cup, almost choking on an unseen watermelon seed. "If your name's Derry, you changed it from Nathan. You're a Jew. And you're no businessman looking for investments. Businessmen looking for investments aren't jumping unannounced into City Hall offices. They're downtown setting up lunches and having lunches set up for them. So, as soon as you finish choking, you can say goodby before you pull whatever you were going to pull on me."

"Hold it," I said, drinking the juice from the fruit cup to stop my spasm. "O.K. I'm not a businessman. My real names's Pevsner."

He nodded with his eyes on me.

"I make my living knowing the difference between a Pole and a Rumanian and a businessman and a con man."

"Democrat?" I guessed.

"Right," he said soberly. "You?"

"Democrat," I said.

"All right, fellow Democrat. Why don't you tell your tale quickly while I digest my lunch."

With nothing better to do while I hid from the cops and nothing much to lose, I told Senator Daley of Illinois my story. He was a damn good listener who threw in two or three questions to be sure I wasn't making it up.

"I'm from a part of Chicago called Bridgeport," he said when I had finished. "It's a tough neighborhood, but it's a good one. When you first came in, I though you were someone I once knew in the Valentine Club from the neighborhood. We were taught not to kill people and not to cheat people. You might have to shake a few hands and a few heads and pull a few deals, but you do what you can in this town and it's a good town. When the Republicans had Chicago with Thompson, people like Capone did what they wanted. Not just with the city but the whole state. The Democrats are changing that. It's not going back the way it was."

He had gradually gotten more and more excited by his little speech, which had started as an explanation to me and moved into a statement to himself and an unseen public. His face flushed and he gave me a lopsided Irish grin.

"The Nittis and Capones and Servis are through," he said. "The gang killing is going to stop. Chicago and Illinois are going to be the best run city and state in—"

"I'm not even a voter," I threw in.

He chuckled, which was better for his digestion than turning red and angry.

"A man who wants to get somewhere in politics has to know when to trust people," he said, wiping his mouth with a napkin. "If he makes too many mistakes, he proves himself a poor judge of character and doesn't deserve the trust and loyalty of others. That's a small campaing speech, but I believe it. Sit still a few minutes and I'll see what I can do."

He left the room and I polished off the roll he had left while I waited. I wasn't sure whether he had decided I was someone to trust or someone not to trust. If I was the latter, a couple of cops would be coming through the door. If I ran now, I might make it out of the building if no one was waiting for me, but I had the feeling that if Daley wanted me to stay he would have taken care to see that I didn't try to run. When he came back in five minutes or so, Daley was smiling. He moved back behind the desk and pulled out his wallet. Before he sat down he handed me his card.

"This isn't my office. I'm just using it for a few days. You can reach me at the number on that card. You've got twenty-four hours to take care of Mr. Marx's troubles," he said. He looked at his watch. "That means you turn yourself in by two o'clock tomorrow afternoon and do what you can to help the police find out who killed those men. The police won't pick you up or bother you til then."

"Thanks," I said. "I'd like to say I'll pay you back some day, but I can't even vote for you."

"That's all right," he grinned. "If you know any Illinois voters, you might suggest that they stick with the Democrats. By the way, I trust you, but I also called a friend with the police department who had records on the case. They don't really think you did it. Trust is one thing. Stupidity is something else. It's a good idea to back up your trust with information."

"Mind if I have that embroidered and hung on my wall?" I said, giving my best pleased grin.

"Be my guest," he said, and added, "If things get a little out of hand and you need a good lawyer, I may be able to make a few suggestions. I've got a law degree from DePaul."

He seemed particularly proud of the last statement, and since it was the only sign of vulnerability he had shown, I nodded in respect.

"One more thing" I said, moving to the door.

"Yes," he said, looking up from his work.

"How do I get to Henrici's?"

"Out the door on Clark Street, north to Randolph and turn right. You can't miss it."

I went out to Clark Street and walked past the cop at the door who had obviously received the word on me. He looked me over to be sure I knew he was looking. I looked back and moved slowly up Clark Street with my hands in my pockets. I found Henrici's. It looked a little fancy but Daley had assured me the special was seventy-five cents. He was right.

By the time I had downed a half dozen scallops, the restaurant was filled with Loop lunchers and I hadn't worked out a better plan. I passed on the fruit cup and had a chunk of orange cake, but that didn't help my thing either. I eyed an almost good-looking secretary downing a tuna on toast at the next table, but she didn't look at me so I left a quarter tip and walked into the cold with my head up.

Two of my difficulties were taken care of. My stomach was full, and the cops and the crooks were giving me a little time.

"You got friends in high places," Kleinhans said.

"Yes, and in medium places too, I hope."

I was calling from a Woolworth's on State Street. In one hand, I had the phone, in the other, a hot dog sandwich. The hot dog was skinny with nothing on it but a little mustard. The phone had more mustard on it than the dog.

"What can I do for you, California?" he said.

"Two things. I've got a meeting set up tonight between Marx and Servi. That should clear Marx, but a thought struck me. What if Servi's the one who's been knocking off the multitudes? What if he pulled this caper on the mob to pick up a clean $120,000?"

"Then he'll just identify Chico Marx as the Chico Marx who owes the mob a lot of money," Kleinhans concluded.

"Right, and Marx either comes up with the money or they start playing games with him and me—games that end with the two of us in small, mailing-size boxes."

"So, why doesn't Marx just pay if it comes to that?"

"Hasn't got the money," I explained, putting the stale hot dog bun down in the phone booth ledge. "His brothers will give it to him, but he's got his own principles. I think he might duck out on a debt or put off paying, but I don't think he'll pay for something he didn't lose."

"So," sighed Kleinhans, "where do I come in?"

"You were assigned to work with me right?"

"Right."

"How about arranging for a little protection in case we have to make a fast exit?"

It seemed reasonable to him. I told him the time and the place of the meeting and suggested that he have a car with a big star parked right in front of the New Michigan Hotel.

"Don't hide it," I said.

A lady of about forty-five, with a white turban and a dead white mink around her neck peered in at me in the phone booth. She looked at her diamond-studded watch, under long black gloves. Then she looked at me. Her teeth were clenched in impatience. I offered her a bite of hot dog through the window. She turned her back on me.

"O.K.," said Kleinhans. "You said there were two things I would do."

"Right, the second is to tell me where in the Loop I can buy an egg. I've gone through four blocks without seeing anything that looked like a grocery."

He asked where I was and told me how to get to a fancy grocery called Smithfield's. He didn't ask me why I needed an egg. I said goodbye to Kleinhans and said I'd turn myself in the next day, as I had promised Daley.

"Take care of yourself, Peters," said Kleinhans, "and don't do anything too stupid."

"It's in my blood," I said. "My brother's a cop."

We both hung up, and the well-dressed lady shoved past me into the booth. I finished my hot dog and made my way to Smithfield's, where I bought a half-dozen eggs. I was tempted to buy a can of quail eggs, too, just to keep on my shelf in L.A. to impress the social register when they dropped by, buy my environment was a dead giveaway, and I didn't want to actually eat quail eggs.

A little after four I went into Kitty Kelly's. Merle was at her table. She gave me a small smile and blew her nose.

"Look what you did," she said, rolling the dice. Her dress was covered with spangles that glittered in the light from the bar. "I'm losing customers from this damned cold you gave me."

She shook her head and kept the small ironic smile to show she didn't mean it, but she did mean it a little, too.

I ordered a beer for myself and a glass of wine and orange juice for her. I did the bit Ian Fleming had pulled at the Fireside. My fingers didn't have his flare. It was a kind of comic parody of what he had done, but it did get a small audience of late afternoon marginal businessmen, two Twenty-One girls and a bartender.

"Drink it," I said. "Old California cure for the common cold."

"You know what you can do with that?" she said.

"Yeah," I answered, "but it wouldn't cure anything that way. Take my word. I've been around doctors a lot recently."

She said "What the hell," downed the orange juice and egg and slugged the wine in two gulps.

"You'll feel better in half an hour," I predicted, and handed her the carton with five more eggs, telling her to use them every two hours.

I purposely lost a few bucks playing Twenty-One and mentioned that I might be getting near the end of my Chicago stay, one way or the other.

"You'll come by and pick up your suitcase, I hope," she said, sounding semitough. "I'm not mailing it to you."

"I though I'd be around at least through the night and you might put me up again."

"I might reinfect you."

"It's worth the risk."

Her smile this time was real, and I asked her how to get in touch with Ray Narducy, the versatile cab driver who had introduced us and did the world's worst Charlie Chan impression. She gave me the number from a book she fished out of her purse, and said he usually went home at dinner time to save a half-buck or so.

"He's a sardine freak," she said. "Eats the stuff every day in sandwiches, salads. He's a good kid, but for a few hours a day he smells like the lake on a hot day when the fish are dying."

After another five minutes of equally intimate

conversation, I squeezed her hand, told her I'd see her later, and made room for a partly plastered businessman who was going to make snappy conversation with a lovely lady while he tried to recover his bar bill.

Narducy was home.

"How'd you like to work for me tonight?" I said. He said he would, and I told him to pick me up in front of the Drake Hotel just before nine. "I'll have the Marx Brothers with me as an added treat."

"I do imitations of all three of them," he said happily. "I even do a Zeppo, but most people don't recognize it."

"Maybe you could skip the impressions tonight. We're going to have things on our mind. Now go back to your sardine sandwich."

"How did you know I was eating sardines?"

"I'm a detective, remember?" I said. "Nine, in front of the Drake."

My wallet told me I had about seventy bucks left. My memory told me I had nothing in the bank. In fact, with my bill from the LaSalle, I was almost minus. I still couldn't take a chance on calling Hoff or Mayer and getting fired. If I held on and the case got wrapped up fast, I had enough to get back to L.A., submit my bill to Mayer, and have a few bucks for some gas and a bag of tacos.

Something resembling sleet pissed cold in my face as I walked in early evening darkness back toward the Drake. I stopped at a coffee shop for a tuna on toast and a Pepsi. I was the only customer. The place was shiny and clean with a steel counter that reflected me from its mirror surface. I tried to ignore myself, ate fast, left a reasonable tip to a waitress who was listening to Smiling Jack on the radio, and continued my journey back to the Drake.

The Marxes had already eaten when I got there. The card game had temporarily ceased, and they were debating the future. I just sat back in a comfortable chair with my hat over my eyes and waited for time to pass.

Every once in a while, I heard them arguing about doing a radio show. I wondered how Harpo would do a radio show, but I minded my own business. Groucho and Chico also argued about doing another movie. Groucho said the script about the department store was awful and couldn't get better. Chico suggested that some things could be done with it.

"You know," he said, "Harp pulls out the harp and gives them a little shit. I play the piano and smile. You push Margaret around and talk to the camera. It always works."

"But it isn't always good," countered Croucho. "What we need is Thalberg back from the dead."

Chico nodded agreement. Harpo said nothing.

"I could sure use the money," sighed Chico.

"What a surprise," Grouch responded.

Business talk went on for another hour. Then there was a pause for nostalgia, with memories of living out on Grand Avenue when they were in Chicago in the old days. They talked about former wives, assorted kids, aunts and uncles.

They spent about two hours talking, beating the extended record I had for conversation with my own brother. Once I had talked to Phil for almost fifteen minutes before he threw a telephone book at me. I'm not sure that time should count though because he was questioning me in his office about a murder.

A little after eight-thirty, I suggested that we get ready. Chico was especially prepared for the event. To meet the gangsters, he had put on a black suit, black shirt, and white tie. Both Groucho and Harpo wore heavy tweeds that looked as if they came off the same racks I used.

Narducy was waiting for us at the curb with his cab. His face was eager, and his neck was straining to look at the three brothers, who sat silently in the back seat. I got in front with Narducy.

Before we pulled away, Narducy turned and surveyed the trio of brothers, deciding which was which. Then, in an Italian accent out of Leo Carillo by way of Henry Armenta, he said: "Hey boss, the garbage mans a here."

"Tell him we don't want any," Groucho shot back.

Then Narducy switched to his Groucho imitation. I elbowed him hard in the ribs before he got very far, but it didn't slow him down.

"Now the next thing we've got in this contract," he said, raising his eyebrows, "is a sanity clause. You know what a sanity clause is, don't you?"

Chico shot back in his now Italian accent: "Take it out. You canta fool me. There's a no Sanity Klaus."

Encouraged by the response, Narducy did a Gookie toward Harp that merited him donations for plastic surgery. Harpo returned the Gookie.

"I like this guy," said Groucho, nodding at Ray,

"but then again, I like cold toilet seats."

"You think we might get moving now?" I said. "Half the underworld is waiting for us."

"And if you do one more imitation of us," added Groucho, "we'll turn you over to these guys and tell them you're Chico."

Narducy started the car with a grin. He pushed his glasses up his nose, narrowly missed a new Nash as he pulled into traffic, turned his voice up to a near falsetto and did an imitation of Kenny Baker singing "Too Blind Love."

Groucho moaned.

Narducy switched to his operatic tenor and tried Allen Jones singing "Alone."

"I give up," cried Groucho. "We'll give give you the $120,000. if you stop."

"Don't pay any attention to him," Chico said. "He always gets this way when he's nervous."

Groucho folded his arms and looked out the window.

As we turned at Michigan and Cermak, I saw the police car Kleinhans promised parked across from the Michigan entrance of the hotel. Narducy pulled his cab around the corner on Cermak and told us the street was named after the mayor who had been assassinated when he took a shot meant for FDR. Cermak, according to Narducy, was a much bigger target. I told him to move far enough down so the cop car couldn't spot him and no one from inside the hotel would know we came in his cab. It might turn out to be safer for all of us.

There was an empty taxi stand a half block away with a little place near it—a shack where you could buy coffee. I told Narducy he could go in there and get a cup, but to be back out in ten minutes in case we had to move fast.

Then the brothers and I got out and walked to the New Michigan. None of them had anything to say. In the lobby they still had nothing to say. Costello was there, and a different night clerk. Some of the ladies who worked out of the place were taking an evening break in the lobby. Chico beamed at a blonde nearby. She beamed back. Groucho caught the exchange of beams and gave Chico a dirty look. Chico shrugged and smiled. Harpo said nothing and looked seriously at the approaching Costello. His arm was still in a sling. His eyes looked at us up and down and across.

"Lift 'em," he said.

I lifted my arms and he frisked me.

"You three, too."

When Costello was satisfied, which took him extra long because he had only one hand to work with and wanted to be sure he didn't make the kind of mistake that had resulted in my getting away from him in Cicero, he nodded for us to go in the elevator.

Chico managed to say something to the blonde, who gave him a deep laugh, a laugh from just above her knees.

"Which one's Chico?" Costello said in the swaying elevator.

"I am," said Chico. Costello gave him a less than friendly look and went silent.

I'd been through this whole thing before. We got out at the same floor, went down the same hall, and found the same Chaney waiting and guarding the door.

"Swordfish," said Groucho.

"Huh?" said Chaney.

"Swordfish," repeated Groucho. "That's the password to get us into this speakeasy. If you don't know your business, you shouldn't be on the door. Chico's had more experience at it than you have."

Chaney's face was blank and confused.

"Never mind," said Groucho. "Forget I said anything. I have a feeling you will anyway."

"He's being funny," Costello explained.

"I don't get it," said Chaney.

It was my turn, and I asked if we could just go in. Chaney opened the door and led us into the same room I had been in before. Costello was behind us. The room had the same furniture, a card table with chairs, a sofa, an old worn easy chair and a picture on the wall of a horse. The big difference was the people. Nitti was in the same chair at the table as if he hadn't moved in days. A heavy-set guy with greying curly hair and a familiar face sat in the easy chair. I figured him for Ralph Capone, but I never found out for sure. Two unfamiliar men stood on either side of the room, far back and silent. One was leaning against the wall, smoking and watching us. The other was just watching us. Their job may have been to hold up the wall, but I had the feeling they were there to back up the curly head in the soft chair. The one person missing from the picture was the one we'd come to see, Gino Servi.

"Who're they?" Nitti said through his teeth, indicating the Marxes.

"Oh," said Groucho stepping forward, "permit me to introduce ourselves. I am Mr. Hardy and this is my friend Mr. Laurel. The gentleman next to him is Edgar Kennedy."

Nobody in the room cracked a smile or gave any indication that they realized Groucho was trying to be funny. Costello had some experience with Groucho and said, "He's being funny, Frank. The talker is Groucho. The one next to him is Chico and the other one is Harpo."

Nitti looked at Groucho, his eyes narrow, and whispered, "Don't talk no more."

Groucho opened his mouth and Nitti's hands clenched, turning red-white.

"Grouch," said Chico. "Don't."

Harpo put a hand on Groucho's shoulder and Groucho shrugged, found a chair, put his elbow on the table and rested his head in his hand.

"Well," said Chico, "Which one is Servi?"

"Not here yet," said Costello. "Soon."

"O.K.," said Chico rubbing his hands together, "How about a couple hands of poker, or—"

I cleared my throat loudly and Groucho groaned. Harpo walked over to look at the picture of the horse.

We sat around for about fifteen minutes, looking at our watches. Chaney and Costello spent some of their time looking at me. The curly-haired guy lifted his hand, and one of the guys near the wall came to him. They whispered. The guy left the room and came back five minutes later with a dark drink with ice for the guy I was sure was Ralph Capone. Nitti looked at him.

"You bring those cops?" said the guy in the soft chair.

"Me?" I said pointing to my chest. "What cops?"

"The ones parked outside," he said calmly, putting away half the liquid in the glass with two swallows. We all watched his Adam's apple.

I didn't say anything more. I didn't know what he knew. Maybe their boys in blue had told them something. If they did, I could lie and get caught. I could tell the truth or say nothing. I kept my mouth shut, and the guy who must have been Capone didn't push it. Ten minutes later he looked restless.

"Where's Servi?" he asked Nitti.

"I don't know. I told him nine. He knows better."

"Can I say something?" said Groucho.

"No," said Nitti.

"Yes," said Capone.

Nitti's head spun toward Capone, who started to get out of his chair. The two boys near the wall moved forward. Costello and Chaney put their hands in their coats. Harpo pretended to keep looking at the horse, which he had been examining steadily for twenty minutes.

Nitti's eyes stayed on Capone and he spoke softly.

"Talk," said Nitti, "but no smart-ass Jew talk."

"This guy Servi's not coming," said Groucho. "He's not coming because he can't identify Chico. He'd walk into this room, look at the three of us and make a wrong guess, because I think this guy Servi helped set you up with a guy imitating by brother."

"The guy who got killed on the West Side yesterday," I threw in. "Old actor named Morris Kelakowsky. I think maybe Servi set it up for him to take you for $120,000. Then he tried to hold Chico up for it."

Nitti rose, glaring from Groucho Marx to me.

Chico just leaned back and watched.

"Sounds possible to me," said Capone.

"Gino's my cousin," said Nitti.

Capone laughed.

"You never heard of a cousin doing in a cousin, or a brother a brother? They may be right, Frank. Gino set all this, got rid of Bistolfi, the Canetta kid and the Jew to keep them from talking."

"Maybe," said Nitti, rubbing his chin.

"If he did," said Capone, "I want him. Bistolfi was working for me."

Capone motioned to Chaney and told him to make some phone calls, to track down Gino. We sat while Chaney reached for the phone and started his calls. He got nervous and turned his eyes down. On the third call, to the Fireside, he got lucky, and kept saying, "Yeah, O.K." He hung up and talked slowly to Nitti.

"Gino left there two hours ago, said he was coming right here. He ain't been home or to any of the other places. You want me to check the hospitals?"

"No," said Nitti.

Capone got up and nodded to the guys against the wall.

"Remember, Frank. I get him."

"We talk to him first," said Nitti.

"Sure," said Capone, "you talk to him. Then I talk to him."

It was my turn.

"Then we can go?"

"You can go back to the Drake and stay there till we find Gino," and Nitti. "Then you get out of town fast if things don't look good for him. We'll let you know."

Groucho was going to say something, but Harpo moved quickly to his side and touched his shoulder, shutting him up. Chico put five bucks on the table, reached down and cut the deck of cards in front of Nitti. Nitti smirked and looked up at him with something that might have been dyspepsia, or grudging respect. Nitti cut the cards. Chico's card was a five of clubs, Nitti's a jack of hearts. Chico led the way out of the door with Costello and Chaney behind us.

When the door closed, we could hear the voices of Capone and Nitti, but couldn't make out the words.

No one said anything on the way down. In the lobby, Chico suggested when he saw the blonde that he might be back at the Drake a little late. I suggested strongly that he do as Nitti said and just go to the hotel.

It had worked out, but not the way I expected. All I had left to do was stick around till the mob nailed Servi. In the morning, I'd tell Kleinhans that Servi was the triple killer. I didn't think the cops would get to him first. Then I'd call Mayer and tell him the whole thing was wrapped up.

The cop car was across the street when we went through the door. Costello followed us out into the wind with his hands in his pockets. He moved his blue face close to me so that I'd be the only one to hear.

"When Frank gives you the word to go," he said without moving his lips, "you got exactly two hours to be out of town and not come back, not ever. Got it?"

"I got it," I said, and led the way around the corner to Narducy's cab. The street was pretty well deserted. The area was mostly industrial. A couple of big factories stood in the sky, silhouetted against the moon. We got in, and Narducy asked how it had gone. The Marxes were quiet. I told Narducy everything looked fine.

We pulled away, and he made a U-turn to take us back to Michigan Avenue. Something bumped in the car and rattled. Narducy said he'd check it later and guessed it was a loose muffler.

We got back to the Drake in ten minutes, and the Marxes got out. I said goodnight and that I'd see them in the morning. Groucho leaned through the door and said "Thanks." No gags, no smirk. No sour face. Harpo shook my hand and grinned, and Chico suggested that he never knew when he might need my help again. I closed the door, and Narducy pulled away singing "Lydia the Tattooed Lady" in his Groucho voice. I didn't mind.

When he pulled in front of his apartment building, I paid him and marked the price and tip in my black book. He said he'd be on the street for a few more hours. I turned to head in and up to Merle while Narducy got out of the cab to check the loose muffler.

About twenty seconds later, he caught me going up the stairs. His eyes were wide and he had something to say, but words weren't coming out, not even an impression of Cary Grant. I followed him back down the stairs and out to the cab.

"Muffler wasn't loose," he finally said, breathing fast in little gulps. "It was the trunk. Someone broke the lock."

He pointed to the trunk and I went over to it. It was partly open. I opened it the rest of the way and found out what had happened to Gino Servi. Someone had put a bullet in his forehead and folded him into Narducy's trunk. Narducy didn't move around to where he could see the corpse again.

"Well?" he said as if he had to find a toilet fast.

"No, not well. Not well at all."

A large caliber bullet had not only cancelled Gino Servi's life but maybe the chance for Chico Marx to walk away clean and me to turn a killer over to the cops.

I was five squares back with nowhere to go, and I was tired, damned tired.

"You got two choices, Raymond," I said, looking down the street to be sure no one was coming or looking. Whoever had given Narducy this present probably knew about me, Narducy, and Merle. Sooner or later he was going to find it easier to get rid of me than to keep sweeping witnesses out of my path. "You go to the cops and tell them you found this gentleman in your trunk, or you dump the body someplace. I suggest you avoid the questions and dump the body."

"I never—" he started. "I can't."

"I have," I said. "And I can. Get back in and tell me a good place to put our friend where the cops can find him."

Ten minutes later, we left Gino sitting on a bench in Lincoln Park looking at a bunch of ice-bound pleasure boats in a harbor. Ten minutes after that Narducy had dropped me at the Ambassador Hotel. He was too nervous to tell if someone had followed us, and I was having too much trouble scheming to worry about it.

The doorman at the Ambassador was tall, black, and polite. He was also young and handsome in a blue uniform. We were a nice contrast on every point. I made my way to the desk walking on a carpet four feet thick. Just off the desk was a restaurant with a sign indicating it was "The Pump Room." Someone opened the door of the Pump Room and I spotted a Negro waiter dressed like Punjab with a big turban. It looked like the kind of place where Ian Fleming would feel at home.

The desk clerk wore a modified tux and was too classy to even give me a suspicious look. He just called Fleming's room and announced me, and Fleming, apparently, said I should come up.

Fleming opened the door with an amused smile on his face, a drink in one hand, and his pearl cigarette holder in the other. He wore a dark smoking jacket that looked as if it were made of velvet. The only other time I had seen anything like it was in a Ricardo Cortez movie a good ten years earlier.

"Mr. Peters," he said genially. "To what do I owe this pleasure? Another attempt on your life?"

He stepped back to let me in, and in I went to a large, carpeted room with plenty of soft furniture and a tall, black-haired woman in a black dress. She looked like an ad for expensive perfume. She didn't look soft like the furniture.

"Were you followed?" Fleming asked matter-of-factly.

"Maybe," I said looking at the woman who raised a drink to her mouth as if she were in a fashion show. The mouth pouted and the face did not show signs of pleasure in my company.

Fleming turned off the hall light behind us and moved quickly to switch off the overhead light in the room, leaving only the light of a table lamp in the corner and the silhouette of the woman.

"I always take rooms on this floor in the Ambassador when I'm in Chicago," Fleming explained. "Someone was overzealous on the doors, and there is a distinct gap between floor and door."

I looked at the door and could see the light from the hall spreading evenly onto the carpet.

"If someone approaches," he explained, "no matter how softly, their shadow will show. Learned that from a Japanese diplomat I was following in New York City last year. Formidable group, the Japanese."

He sat comfortably in the chair after smoothing his smoking jacket behind him and asked me if I wanted a drink. I passed, and tried not to look at the tall woman. Fleming acted as if she were not there and might have gone on ignoring her had she not cleared her throat.

"Ah, yes, Mr. Peters, this is Prosephone Fabrikant, a not very old and not yet a dear friend."

The woman winced at both the phoney name and the comment, but said nothing.

"I'm sorry to—"

"Don't apologize," Fleming said quickly. "Our last meeting was the most exhilarating event of recent years. Perhaps our second can evoke the memory."

"Are you going to be tied up long?" sighed Prosephone Fabrikant in an accent distinctly cultured and distinctly American, probably Boston.

Fleming looked at me with an eyebrow raised.

"I was hoping you could put me up for the night," I said.

Prosephone Fabrikant's irritation reverberated from the walls and shot right through me.

"Of course," said Fleming. "Prosephone and I can continue our discussion tomorrow." He looked at her with confidence coming dangerously close to indifference. She tried to stare him down icely, but she was no match for a man who had practiced that look for long hours before a mirror, or else was just born to it. If I tried it, I'd look like a punch-drunk middleweight who heard bells when there were no bells.

"Of course," she said, finally putting down her drink and stalking to the door. Fleming rose to follow her, but he didn't hurry and he was right. She hesitated with her hand on the knob, and I retreated as discretely as I could to the window to look out at the lights of downtown Chicago.

I couldn't make out the words, but her voice sounded hurt and weak—a voice that seemed out of place in that cool body. His voice was firm but soft. He kissed her for a long time, but without frenzy or fire. Then he opened the door, guided her out, and closed it behind her.

"Met her in the bar downstairs," Fleming said, returning to the room. "Don't really remember her name, but have the distinct impression from her ring that she is married. Toby, women are not to be trusted—but American women, for all their deceit, are a distinctly superior lot to Englishwomen. English-women simply do not wash and scrub enough."

I shrugged and told my tale. At last I began to tell my tale. When I was about to tell him about Servi's body in the park waiting for sunrise, he rose and put his finger to his lips. He nodded to the door, and I could see a distinct shadow blocking out a chunk of light in the hall. Fleming made an opening and closing motion with his hand to indicate that I should continue talking. I did while he made his way slowly to the door. He was within a foot of the door when an ancient floorboard under the carpeting gave him away with a distinct creak. The shadow snapped away from the door and footsteps clopped down the hall. Fleming jerked the door open and disappeared. I was a few feet behind him.

Fleming had ten years on me and I remembered him telling me something about having been an athlete. He made a strange looking sprinter in his velvet smoking jacket and slippers, but he was a fast son-of-a-bitch. I couldn't keep up with him. He went through an exit door and I followed about fifteen feet behind. When I went through the door I stopped to listen for footsteps. My heavy breathing got in the way, but I managed to control it long enough to determine that people were running up the stairs, not down. I went up. Down would have been more fun.

About four flights up I heard a metal door open and close with a clang. Then it opened and closed again. A second or two later I thought I heard a shot. By the time I reached the metal door at the top of the stairway, I hoped there was no one beyond it waiting for me. I needed a week or two to get my legs back and inhale enough air to stay alive. It was either age or the flu or both, or maybe just good sense, but I was tired. I was also responsible for a partly mad Englishman who might be getting shot at by a guy who knew how to shoot.

I pushed the door open and got hit in the face by a blast of wind from the lake. I waited for the wind to pass, but it didn't. The roof of the Ambassador in the winter was not the ideal place for shelter.

The moon was partially out and I could make out the shapes of chimneys and air ducts, but I couldn't see any people. I did hear the shot that tore up a spray of snow at my feet. I jumped into the darkness behind a chimney and tripped over a body.

"Fleming?"

"Fleming the fool, at your service," he said tightly. "I have a very neat little Barretta in my suitcase—oiled, clean, dying to be used."

"Sorry," I said, waiting for the man we had trapped to figure out we were unarmed and come looking for us. My eyes adjusted to the near light and I looked at Fleming who, in spite of the thin jacket, didn't look in the least cold. The only effect of the last ten minutes had been to mess up his hair. As if sensing this, he reached up and patted it neatly in place.

"I wonder," he said, "if there is another way down from here."

"I don't want to try it," I said.

"No, no old chum, I wasn't worried about our escape. I don't want our elusive friend to scamper."

Something crunched in the snow about twenty

feet away. The howl of the wind mixed with the sound, but both Fleming and I heard it. We looked at each other. I'm sure the fear was clear in my eyes. He looked positively happy.

"Good, now we know where he is," he whispered, and pointed to the right while he slipped away into the darkness on the left. I crawled where he had indicated as quietly as I could, but it wasn't good enough. Another shot hit too close to me to be luck. I crawled fast, rolling for cover behind a ridge of brick. Both my heart and the footsteps were about equal in volume and both were getting louder. He couldn't have been more than a dozen feet from me when whoever it was let out a pained grunt. Less then a second later the footsteps retreated. I peered over the ridge of bricks cautiously and saw the faint outline of a man about thirty feet away. He took two more shots into the darkness, and I screwed up my courage and stood up.

"This is the police," I shouted making my voice as deep and as loud as I could. "Step out here with your hands over your head. Murphy," I said in a stage whisper, "if anyone comes in view with a gun in his hand, start shooting and ask questions later."

Not having thought out the consequences of this move I wondered what I would do if someone did step forward with a gun in hand and saw me unarmed. I hurried in a crouch to a metal air duct and was rewarded by the sound of hurrying feet and the slam of the metal door. Just in case it might be a trick, I sat for another shivering minute or two and then made a circle to the door. I pulled it open and found nothing.

Then I began to search for Fleming's velvet-clad

body. By leaning forward, I managed to follow a maze of foot prints in the snow in a variety of circles. One set of prints, however, led to a nauseating end at the edge of the building. I didn't want to look over and down. A few months earlier, in Los Angeles, I had seen a midget take an enforced dive out of a high window—and one sight like that in a man's life is one more than he needs. I rubbed a ball of snow in my face and leaned over into the blast of wind.

The fingers of a pair of hands stood out distinctly no more than two feet below, clinging to a concrete design in the hotel.

"Fleming?" I called into the wind though it didn't take much to realize it couldn't be anyone else.

"Peters," he said somewhat faintly, but without fear—at least without fear I could detect. "Glad you found me. It's rather difficult to hold on and I really don't see how I can scramble up."

I leaned over with one hand on the brick ridge of the roof and watched while one of Fleming's slippers dropped from his foot and went sailing down into the night, flickering past lighted windows to disappear far below. Fleming's face was hidden by the jutting of concrete, but I could see his body literally swaying in the stiff wind. I eased my way out, trying not to lose my frosty grip with my left hand while my not-long-enough right arm inched down to Fleming's fingers.

"Don't let go til I have a grip on your wrist," I shouted.

He responded, but I couldn't make out the words. I did manage to get a reasonably good grip on his left wrist, but the whole operation was full of potential failure. My hands were cold and so were his, and I didn't know if I had the strength to pull him up even if I could hold my grip.

"Don't try to pull," he shouted. "Just get a firm grip and let me try to get up on your arm."

He let go with both hands and my left arm pulled painfully in the socket, but I held my grip. His right hand reached up to get a grasp on my sleeve and he threw his legs up agilely over the same concrete outcroping to which he had been clinging. Just as my right hand lost its hold on the moist wrist, Fleming's left hand grabbed the brick along the roof and he pulled himself up and over.

We lay there panting and enjoying the firmness beneath us for a minute or two without speaking.

"Do things like this happen to you often?" he finally gasped.

"Sometimes," I said.

"Fascinating," he came back with a grin. He pulled himself up and helped me to my feet. "I hope you don't resent my saying this Toby, but aren't you getting a bit long of tooth for this sort of thing?"

I shrugged and he nodded in understanding.

As we made our way down the stairs back to his room, Fleming explained that he had heard the man with the gun take a shot at me and had, in turn, thrown a snowball with a rock in it at the carrier of certain doom. The man, whom he did not get a decent look at, had turned and taken a few shots at him, and Fleming had scrambled over the side of the roof to avoid the bullets.

"I don't think anyone heard the shots with the wind

blowing like this," I said, as we went into the room and Fleming closed the door behind us.

He kicked off his remaining slipper, finished off his bourbon and branch water while humming a tune I didn't recognize, and went into the bedroom to get his gun.

"We must stay in touch," he said, turning an armchair to face the door. "Now I suggest you lie down on the sofa and get a few hours sleep while I tell you my life's story."

I was too tired to argue so I kicked my shoes off and stretched out. The last thing I remembered him saying was that he had either studied under a psychiatrist in Austria or been studied by one. Either possibility seemed reasonable to me at that point.

In my dream, Cincinnati was undergoing a massive reconstruction and I kept having to move from house to house to stay out of the way. I'd had the dream before and I didn't like it. When I woke up in the morning, Fleming was sipping a cup of coffee. He wore a fresh suit and was clean shaven.

"Sleep well?" he said.

"O.K.," I said.

Fleming looked at his watch. "I have an appointment or two," he said, "and I think you have a crime to get on with."

We shook hands.

"If you ever get to L.A., look me up," I said. "I'm in the phone book."

"And if you ever get to England after this damned war of ours, look me up."

I went out the door without looking back, made it

to the lobby without being shot, let the doorman get me a cab, and told the cabbie Merle's address.

In the very late morning, I shaved, made a couple of scrambled eggs and some toast for Merle and threw two more eggs on for Narducy, who stopped in. Merle coughed her way through breakfast and put up a half-hearted resistance to the orange juice I forced on her. Narducy just looked at his coffee and pulled out a copy of the *Chicago Times*, a tabloid with a little line drawing of a camera looking at the reader at the top of the page.

Merle had a half box of Rice Krispies on a high shelf, which wasn't so appetizing, but she also had two brown bananas, which compensated. I had three bowls of Krispies with bananas and read about Servi being found on the Lincoln Park bench frozen solid. The story was on page four with no picture. My tale of murder and machine-gunning, under O'Brien's by-line, made page three with one-column shots of Bistolfi, Canetta, Morris Kelakowsky, and me. The photo of me was the worst, which seemed unfair since I was the only one of the quartet still alive. They had dug up an employment photo from my Glendale police days and had it sent by wire. It was a good ten years old. As awful as I felt, I knew I looked a lot better than that right now.

O'Brien played up the fugitive bit and added a little more blood to my already bloody tale. Aside from that, and the strong indication that I was responsible for the murders, the story seemed fair enough.

"I fixed the lock and cleaned out the trunk," Narducy muttered.

Merle wandered dizzily back to the bedroom in her floppy robe and groaned.

"Toby," she croaked in a voice two octaves lower than I recognized, "take care of yourself."

"Well, Raymond," I said, rinsing out dishes, "I've got two hours to turn myself in to the cops."

"Hell," he said, "you can just get on a bus or train and get out of here. The paper says they just want you for questioning. They wouldn't drag you back from California, would they?"

"I don't think so, but I promised a guy I'd turn myself in. I haven't got much to sell but a body that's ready for scrap, a brain that doesn't work half the time, and my word. I can't count on the body and brain, but my word has held up pretty well."

Narducy shrugged and threw down the last two scrambled eggs and a slice of toast.

"How about finishing up and getting me over to the

Drake so I can give the bad news to the Marx Brothers?"

Narducy nodded, finished eating everything on the table that could be eaten, put on his jacket and cap, inched his glasses up, and said he was ready. I looked in on Merle, who was asleep and giving off rasping sounds.

The sun was high, but nothing was melting as we went through the streets. I tried to think, but I was out of tricks and ideas. Narducy said he'd wait for me while I talked to the Marxes. Costello and Chaney were in the Drake lobby not even pretending to hide behind a newspaper. I walked over to them

"Marx don't leave," said Costello. "Not till Frank finds out what happened to Gino. You don't leave either till Frank says."

"Someone's been reading the papers," I said.

"That a crack about my being able to read?" said Costello through his teeth.

"No," I reassured him, "I'm not in the crack-making business today. I've got more important things to do."

"Like?"

"Like keeping somebody alive," I said, and walked to the elevator.

The Marxes were dressed and arguing, at least Groucho and Chico were arguing. Harpo was doodling on a pad.

"Well, Peters," said Groucho, "you got more publicity in Chicago today than we had all last year."

"In my business, publicity is not a sign of success," I said.

I hadn't sat down, and Chico invited me to pull up

a chair. I did and the three brothers looked at me.

"You've got something to say, Peters," said Chico.

"Yeah, Nitti's boys are downstairs, and Nitti's not a patient man. I've got to turn myself in to the Chicago cops in an hour about those killings, and I don't think they'll let me go for a while. I don't know who killed those guys, and I don't know who set Chico up as the fall guy. I'm no closer than I was five days ago. The only changes are that I've managed to get four guys killed and to give pneumonia to a lovely lady. My advice to you," I said, looking at Chico, "is to borrow the $120,000 from your brothers, give it to Nitti, and go back to California."

"O.K.," said Chico. "Then what do you do?"

"Cops hold me a few days, and I keep trying to find out who killed those guys. Maybe I get lucky and it ties in to who set you up. I think it will."

"And what does Nitti say about your staying around?" asked Groucho.

"I don't think he'll like it, but I've never been very good at keeping friends."

"One more bit of feeling sorry for yourself and we'll call Nitti and have him cart you out of here right now," said Groucho.

"Whoever's pulling all this is always a step ahead and inside my mind. It might take me forever to catch him, or them," I said.

"Who knew?" said a voice.

I didn't recognize the speaker. At first I thought someone had come through the door or the radio was on, but the door was closed, and the Arvin on the table was dark and cold.

"Who knew where you were going? Who did you tell?"

The voice came from Harpo. It was the first time I had heard him speak since I met him. I looked at Groucho and Chico, but they didn't find speech from their brother worthy of comment.

"What?" I said, looking at him. His voice had been soft, almost as if he were speaking to himself.

"Did you tell anyone where you were? Anyone who knew each place you went?"

"Somebody may have been following me," I said, "but the killer was ahead of me on the West Side, and—" Then I got the idea. It seemed good, and then it seemed stupid, and then it seemed good again. There was only one thing wrong with it, one thing that didn't make sense.

"Can I use your phone for a long distance call?"

"Be our guest," said Chico.

I got the operator and placed the call to Miami. It took me and the operator about ten minutes to reach the person I wanted, but when I got him I asked him one question. The answer told me who my killer was.

"Well?" said Groucho. "You look like the cat who swallowed Kitty Carlisle."

"I've got less than an hour to turn myself in to the cops," I said. "I think you can start packing and stop worrying about that $120,000. I'll give you a call or be back later."

In the lobby I stopped to have a talk with Costello. He said he'd have to check with Nitti about what I wanted, but he'd call right away.

Narducy was reading a detective magazine when I got in the cab.

"Know where the Maxwell Street Police Station is?" I said.

He did, and we shot into traffic going south.

If it weren't so close to two, I probably would have gone back to Merle's for my .38. I've thought about it a couple of times. It would have changed things, probably a lot, but I'm not sure it would have been better.

We hit Twelfth Street and headed east, turned left at an old church, and pulled up in front of a dirty, three-story brick police station that looked like a good man in a bulldozer could level it in five minutes.

"Don't wait," I said, paying Narducy off. "This may take a while." He nodded and drove off.

My watch said it was two minutes to two when I walked up the worn stone steps and pushed open the door.

My picture had been on page three of the *Chicago Times*, and probably in the *Tribune*. It was also posted, I was sure, in the Maxwell Street Police Station. Granted that the picture didn't resemble me, there must have been a pretty good description going. Nobody in the station grabbed me.

There was an old cop on the desk. His face looked like Death Valley. He was in agony over a crossword puzzle he was working on with a well-sharpened pencil, and didn't look up when I asked for Kleinhans. He directed me through a door marked "Squad Room."

The Squad Room was a high-ceilinged wreck stained with years of things that come from human bodies—things like tears, vomit, and tobacco juice. It smelled of heavy, ancient sweat. There were four desks and a long table in the room. At the long table, a little man who looked like an insurance salesman, except for his shoulder holster, was patiently going through a mug book with a serious-looking young guy in a brown wool jacket.

The insurance salesman cop was saying, "Are you sure, Mr. Castelli? The man you just identified is Tony Accardo. I don't think he'd be likely to con you out of five bucks on a street corner."

"I think it's him," said Castelli.

"Let me put it to you this way, Mr. Castelli," said the insurance cop, "if I thought Accardo conned you, I'd be happy to pull him in, but I don't think he did, and I think I should tell you he's not a con man. He's a mobster."

"I'm probably wrong," said Castelli, looking at the picture again.

"Probably," said the cop. "Let's look at some more."

They looked at some more, and I looked around the room for Kleinhans. A cop at one desk was typing a report and singing "Shine on Harvest Moon." His hair was clipped short, and he had a red bull neck with bristles on it that rubbed against his collar. The woman sitting at the chair near his desk wasn't singing. She was holding on to her purse with two hands and trying to read what the cop was typing. She looked like a scared bird or Zasu Pitts. At another desk, three cops were looking at something in a folder and laughing. It was loud dirty laughter. I felt at home. It was like most of the police stations and precinct houses I had been in and out of since I was twenty.

Kleinhans was seated at the desk furthest back, near a drafty window covered with bars and so dirty you couldn't see through it. It was the choice location in the room. Kleinhans saw me before I saw him. He was talking to a thin man with a day's growth of beard, and a brown hat that had gone mad trying to keep its shape. It may have been driven over the brink by the hole in the crown that looked like it came from a bullet. The thin man's hands were moving furiously in explanation, anguish, pain, and plea bargaining.

Kleinhans smiled at me, and I walked over to him, catching the end of the thin man's sentence.

"—so what use would I have for such a thing like that?"

"I don't know, Sophie," said Kleinhans. "Maybe you can ask the judge that."

"Aw, Sergeant," the thin man said, his eyes filling with tears, "you're not going to turn me over for a couple of pair of shoes? Left-footed soccer shoes. What the hell? The lock-up's cold, Sergeant, and with my bursitis—"

"You win," said Kleinhans, holding up his hand. "Your tale touched my heart, Soph. Those tears won me over. Get out of here, and don't let me see you on the street for a month."

The thin man fell into shock. His mouth dropped open. He looked at Kleinhans and then at me, but he didn't move.

"I—I—I can just go?" he said. "No booking? You ain't even going to rough me a little?"

Kleinhans shook his head.

"Naw, Soph, you're little fish on the street today.

This man's public enemy number one." He pointed at me, and Soph's eyes turned up in confusion and awe. "Wanted in connection with four murders in the last week, and he's turning himself over to me. What do you think about that?"

"It's nice," said the thin man, removing his battered hat, crumpling it and putting it on again.

"Right," said Kleinhans, "and I don't have time to write you up Soph, so move. Don't say thanks, just move and remember you owe me."

A smile twitched on Sophie's face as he got up quickly and headed for the exit. He nearly hit Zasu Pitts, and she clutched her purse tighter as he dashed out the door.

"Have a seat, Peters," said Kleinhans. "Want a cup of coffee?"

Not only couldn't you see through his window, but the thin draft knifed across the desk. Kleinhans' concession to the chill was a brown sweater over his shirt and tie. The sweater had a small hole on the right arm.

"No coffee," I said.

"Well," he said, stretching and putting his hands behind his neck, "you decided to make me a hero by turning yourself in to me. I appreciate that. It'll take me off the desk for the day."

"I haven't had lunch," I said. "Someplace we can go for a sandwich and some talk?"

"O.K.," he said, getting up and putting on his coat. "I'll introduce you to the best hot dog in the world."

Kleinhans told one of the three laughing cops to watch his desk because he was going out to lunch. The cop nodded and turned back to the folder.

A uniformed cop stopped Kleinhans as we hit the Squad Room door. He wanted to know where he should put someone, or something, called Verese. Kleinhans looked toward the cop singing "Shine on Harvest Moon" and indicated that Verese should go to him.

On the street, the sun was shining and the wind was calm. The temperature had shot up to the very low thirties. I'd been in Chicago less then a week but it seemed like a balmy day to me. With his hands in his pockets, Kleinhans turned right on Maxwell Street and looked straight ahead. A cop car pulled up and Kleinhans nodded to the two guys who got out.

"Ever been on Maxwell Street?" said Kleinhans.

"No," I said, "is it something to remember?"

He shrugged. Within half a block, the street was crammed with pushcarts. Some of them were as long as two Chevies, some were covered with canvas, but most were open for business with men, women, and boys hawking goods to each other and to bundled-up customers. The cars lined both sides of the two-way street and narrowed the area for driving to barely a car's width. Behind the pushcarts, on either side of the street, were shops and stores with more men, women, and boys talking to passersby, shifting their legs to stay warm as they caught a potential customer, or lost him and went for a new one.

Signs were all over the place—hand-lettered, some with cartoons on them, some in Yiddish. The spelling was awful. The cardboard they were written on was flimsy, but the bargains were terrific providing you could use lots of slightly warped arrows, soiled suitcases, sox—pairs and nots—rope, screwdrivers with handles melted by a railroad fire, army pillows, suits—"perfect."

"This bargain day?" I said.

"No," said Kleinhans, "this is an off day, a slow weekday afternoon. You should come on a Sunday."

The air smelled as if everything on sale had been grilled in onions—sweet and just this side of nauseating. A thin kid no more than thirteen, who should have been in school, grabbed my arm and shouted in my face:

"Ties, ties! Yours got dirt all over. Look at these ties." He held up a handful of ties that looked like they were stolen from the Ringling Brothers clowns during intermission.

"Sorry," I said. The kid was going to try again, but he saw Kleinhans and recognized him. The kid turned to another prospect.

Then Kleinhans grabbed my arm, grinned and pointed across the street. We moved between two carts and in front of a grey Buick that was inching its way up the street. I wondered what would happen if a car came the other way.

The small cart in the middle of the block was a white square with a hot dog painted on the side. The paint was peeling, and the dog had begun to show blue under the red.

"Tony's gonna be famous some day," said Kleinhans, ordering two dogs "with everything." Tony was a little round man with a dark face, an apron, and a serious professional look.

"I'll take ketchup instead of mustard," I said, "and no peppers."

Tony nodded, businesslike, and worked with a flourish.

Kleinhans handed me a hot dog sandwich wrapped in a napkin and gave Tony two quarters.

"On me," he said.

A shot of wind came along, and Kleinhans pointed to a doorway with his hot dog. He had already taken a bite out of it that reduced the sandwich by a third.

In the doorway, I took a bite and admitted it was a damn good dog.

"You want to talk business?" I asked with a mouthful of dog and onion. There were little seeds on the bun, and it was hot and soft. Kleinhans' mouth was full, and a mustard-covered onion fell from it as he nodded that talking was all right with him.

"I think I know who killed Servi and the others," I said.

He nodded and kept eating.

"At least," I went on, "I know who killed Servi and I have a pretty good idea who killed the others."

"Who?" he said, chomping down the last bit of his sandwich. "I think I'll get another one. You want a second?"

"Not through with my first," I said, "but it is the best dog I ever ate. Don't you want to know who the killer is?"

"I said, 'Who?', didn't I?" he said, cleaning his fingers with the napkin and throwing it toward the sidewalk where it hit a Mexican woman walking by.

"You," I said, pausing on my way to indigestion.

Kleinhans looked at me and shook his head.

"No," I said. "I mean it. Harpo Marx gave me the idea. I should have figured it out, but I kept putting the idea away. Too much coincidence. Then I asked myself whether it was coincidence."

"I don't get it," said Kleinhans.

"When you met me at the station the day I arrived," I explained, "you said your boss had sent you to work with me. I figured your boss was a cop who had a call from the Miami police, possibly an overly-conscientious county cop named Simmons. Otherwise who could have called your boss? I called Simmons this morning. He didn't call anyone in Chicago about my coming. He checked around and none of his people called. The way I figure it, Bistolfi called someone in Chicago, probably Servi, to say I was on my way. Then Servi got in touch with you and told you to stick with me. Should I keep going or you want to give me some help?"

Kleinhans kept smiling. "Go on," he said.

"I talked to one of Nitti's boys this morning and asked if he knew a cop named Kleinhans. He didn't say, but he got quiet fast. The way I figure it, you were in on this with Servi, working for him, giving him protection. Then he got the idea of taking Nitti and the mob for a bundle and let you in on it. He needed you to keep any investigation from starting. If Nitti smelled something, Servi would suggest that you look into it. Since you were already part of the deal, you'd find nothing or a fall guy. Everything looked good. Morris won a bundle."

"Won and lost," corrected Kleinhans. "He played five different places on Chico Marx's tab. He lost 120 grand and almost won 100 grand. He took the $100,000 in cash from the places he won and left markers for the $120,000 he lost."

"Thanks," I said.

Kleinhans shrugged.

"What the hell. You gotta take risks sometimes to make a buck."

"Bistolfi figured out what was going on and wanted a piece of it?" I guessed. Kleinhans nodded.

"But there wasn't enough yet to make splitting worthwhile," he said. "And Bistolfi had ties to Capone. It wasn't worth the risk."

"So you gunned him in my room?"

Kleinhans nodded yes.

"We thought a stiff might send you back to California."

"Why didn't you just put some holes in me?" I said.

"Besides the fact that I liked you," he said, looking out and waving at a pair of old men who walked by, "it wouldn't have done much good. Whoever paid you could have paid another private cop who might be even smarter than you. No. Servi figured the way to go was to get rid of anyone who could lead you to us."

"Makes sense," I agreed.

Kleinhans chuckled deep.

"Almost made a mistake with you, though," he said, blowing his nose. "I sent you to Canetta's place on the West Side and came damn near not beating you there. I got called in to identify a guy after I called you. Had to really move my ass to get there ahead of you. You almost made it a tie."

"You took a shot at me."

He laughed.

"If I wanted to hit you, I would have done it when you came in the door. We didn't want you dead if we could help it. We just wanted you tied up as a suspect."

"Canetta tried to tell me you shot him. He said 'cop.' I think he was trying to tell me a cop or cops shot him. I thought he wanted me to get the cops."

"See what I mean about a smarter private eye?" said Kleinhans.

"Yeah, I wasn't very smart about Servi," I said. "I told you I had the meeting set up with Servi and Marx. You knew Servi couldn't bluff his way through it. If Servi went down, you'd go down, as you waited for Servi at the New Michigan—"

"No," he said. "I picked him up at the Fireside and drove him to the New Michigan. I pulled up behind your cab. The kid wasn't in it. I put one between Gino's eyes, pried open the cab trunk, dumped him in, and followed you to the Ambassador."

We didn't say anything else for a minute or so. It looked as if everything had been said.

"You know what a cop's home is like in Chicago?" he said.

"You're not looking for sympathy, are you, Kleinhans?"

"Hell no," he said. "I'm explaining. You know what it's like to have a kid brother who's up to his ass in money from business deals while you don't make enough to pay the milkman? Ever been offered a second rate job by your own brother? I've had blood on my suit and had to scrape it off and douse it in cold water because I couldn't pay the cleaning bill. I've got four kids. One in college. One who's deaf. You know what all that costs?"

"Enough to make you kill four people?"

"Those weren't people, Peters. They were garbage. Bistolfi was a cheap triggerman. Servi was covered in other people's blood. Canetta was a knife who picked pockets. He got in the way. When Bistolfi told us you were on the train, I called Canetta in Jacksonville, where he was running an errand for Servi. He wanted to put a knife in you on the train."

I remember being asleep next to Canetta on the train. Now I knew he had been dreaming of putting a blade through my only suit.

"What about Morris Kelakowsky?" I said. "He a killer, too?"

Kleinhans shrugged.

"He knew what he was getting into."

"I doubt it," I said.

"I've got a couple for you, Peters. What the hell did you go to the mayor's for?"

"Something a smarter private cop wouldn't have done. I wanted to put some pressure on City Hall with promises from Hollywood. I figured a right word would get you and the Chicago cops off my back while I saved Chico. It was dumb. Not the dumbest thing I've ever done, though. My ex-wife thinks I do things like that because I like to live dangerously. Makes me feel alive. That's why she left me. Or one reason, anyway."

"Maybe she's right," Kleinhans suggested. "Look what you just did. You walked right into my doorway. You could have gone to your local police station or to one of the guys who pulled the strings to get you time yesterday."

"I'd rather think she's right than I'm stupid."

"I said I had a couple of things," Kleinhans said, looking toward the street. "You want the other one?"

"Shoot," I said. And he did.

The bullet ripped through the last piece of sandwich in my hand and hit me in the side. The sound wasn't too loud. A few people looked toward us, but Kleinhans reached over and held me up like we were old pals. I was looking down at a bloody hot dog and a dark wet hole in my jacket.

"Some people get too clever, Toby," he whispered. "Knew a guy who shot his brother in the eyes when he was sleeping. Small caliber gun. Then he closed the eyes and said he died in his sleep. Coroner almost didn't open the eyes. It was a busy day, and he was ready to accept the family doctor's statement of heart attack. I found the holes when I looked."

"Very interesting," I said, fighting back the taste of blood.

"Another time," he said softly, "I went to a funeral. Suicide. Something to do with the Genna Brothers, back when I was in uniform. Bullet right in the head. You know what was funny? The corpse was wearing gloves. I pulled off the gloves and found bullet holes through both palms. He'd put up his hands when someone shot him. Someone was his wife. You see where I'm taking you, Peters?"

"Yeah," I gasped. "Keep it simple."

"Right," he said, giving me a pat on the shoulder. I

could feel the barrel of the pistol being pushed against my chest as he moved close to me and turned me away from the street.

I shoved the bloody hot dog bun in his face, let myself fall backward on the sidewalk, knocked over a pair of young winos, and rolled under a cart. My face scrapped the street bricks, and my hand touched something soft. I kept rolling onto the street.

Kleinhans had turned in the doorway. He leveled the gun at me. A guy selling shoes in the cart saw the gun, muttered "shit" and pushed his fat female customer away. I was on my knees, my back against a Dodge stuck in traffic. A woman screamed. Someone shouted something in a language I had never heard before.

"You shouldn't have tried that," shouted Kleinhans. His second shot would have hit me in the chest if the guy in the Dodge hadn't panicked when he saw Kleinhans. He lurched forward, stripping gears, and sent me spinning ten feet down the street.

I made it to my feet and looked back. The street was crowded with people running out of the way and into each other. He might have hit one of them instead of me. I doubted if he cared, but I also doubted that he'd want to have to explain.

My side felt hot, but I knew I had something left for running. I also knew from our chase on the West Side that I was at least a little faster than Kleinhans. I knew I wasn't faster than his gun, but I might find someplace to hide or a cop to give myself up to before he caught me.

I hit a cart full of sweet corn and crashed into a

street sign that said I had hit the corner of Maxwell and Halsted. People scattered like the Red Sea when they saw me staggering down the sidewalk. They opened further when they say Kleinhans behind me with his gun. A man in front of a store selling chickens must have been deaf and near blind. He grabbed my arm and said something about two live chickens for the price of one. He shoved two live kicking chickens in my face. I pulled away from him and lost a little distance between Kleinhans and me. I was also losing blood.

Over my shoulder, I could see Kleinhans shrugging off the blind chicken salesman. I pushed past a woman who looked like a gypsy and fell on my ass into a store, hoping I had lost Kleinhans. From the floor, I could see I was surrounded by cheap chalk statues of Christ on the cross. They hovered over me, shining and long. Chalk madonnas stood between them, looking past me with smiling baby Jesus's in their arms. I inched back toward the walls, looking for shadow or cover. My head hit the feet of a big plaster Jesus crucified on the wall.

There was a heavy counter to my right. I scurried behind it like a de-winged beetle just as the door of the shop opened and closed. I could hear Kleinhans' heavy breathing and see his body distorted through the counter glass.

"You left a trail of blood, Toby," he said aloud.

I knew the trail led down the counter and around to me. I didn't have the strength or the room to run. I got to my knees, trying not to breathe, when he came to the front of the counter. The next step would be for him to lean over and blow a hole in my head. My hand touched something smooth and waxy. I turned and saw a three-foot high wax candle of Our Lady of Guadalupe. There were four just like her in a row. As Kleinhans hand shook the counter to balance himself, I stood up with one of the wax candles in both hands and swung at his leaning head with everything I had. A bullet shattered the counter. The candle statue's head flew across the room and Kleinhans, stunned, fell back against a display table.

What I needed next was enough strength to hit him again with something hard that would put him out. I threw the rest of the candle at him, but it missed. He was on one knee when the door opened. Kleinhans turned toward it with his gun up, but Costello was ready. From his pocket, he put three bullets in the cop.

"Where the hell were you?" I said, watching him go out of focus.

"You said Maxwell Street," Costello said. "You didn't say where on Maxwell Street."

"Terrific," I said.

"Yeah," he said, going right back out the door. He didn't even wave his slinged arm as he pushed through the crowd. No one tried to stop him.

Kleinhans was sprawled with one knee out and his dead, surprised eyes examining a spot of blood on the floor. People crowded to the door of the shop, faces pressed to the glass of the window. A few hundred eyes were looking at me and fogging the glass. I was getting smaller and smaller, turning into a trained flea in a bottle everyone was looking at. I had no tricks for them. The door was open, but none of them came in.

I think I remember a cop in blue pushing the door

open and pointing a gun at me. I think I remember a guy from the crowd coming over to me and talking about the A & P basketball team.

"We've got to play on hardwood floors," the guy groaned, telling me to sit down.

"I can't sit down," I said. "I've been shot."

"I don't know if we can play on hardwood floors," the guy said.

"Don't worry," I said. "It'll be all right."

When I opened my eyes, I was looking at a nine-year-old kid with thick glasses and black hair that kept falling forward. He told me he was a doctor and I was in the emergency room of Cook County Hospital.

"How long have I been out?" I asked.

"I wouldn't worry about that, Mr. Peters," he said, patting my shoulder. "You've been shot—we don't think seriously, but—"

"Get me a phone," I said. Something like pain was knitting a sweater out of my insides.

His smile was tolerant but put-upon.

"I'm sorry," he said. "There'll be plenty of time for that—"

I made it up on one elbow and spoke as quietly and clearly as I could.

"You get me a phone or you don't cut me open."

"You can't—"

"Get me a phone or I cut you open," I tried.

"I'm here to help you," he said, turning pale.

"Good, then help me by getting a phone or getting me to one."

"I don't see how—"

This time he was interrupted by a Negro woman in white who outweighed him by thirty pounds and probably outexperienced him by the same number of years.

"I think we should let him make the call, doctor," the nurse said. "Arguing with him isn't getting us anywhere. Now Mister," she said to me, "Who do you want to call?"

The child doctor looked like he was going to protest, but settled for throwing out his hairless jaw and muttering, "What the hell?" as he stalked away.

"Don't mind him," the nurse said to me, pushing the cart I was on to a corner. "He's been working for twenty-four hours."

"He doesn't even need a shave," I said.

"Who do you want to call?" she said.

"In my wallet pocket, there's a card with the name Daley on it."

I wasn't wearing my suit, but she fished my bloody pants out of a metal locker and found the card. She called the number and asked for Daley.

"This is Mr. Peter's secretary," she said and handed me the phone.

"Daley?" I asked. "This is Peters."

"Yes," he said. "You turned yourself in?"

"I did," I said.

"You sound strange," he said. "Hurt?"

"I'm in the hospital. I'll be all right. I got shot by a crooked cop named Kleinhans, Sergeant Charles Kleinhans, Maxwell Street Station. Got that?"

"I've got it," he said.

"Kleinhans is dead. Shot by a mob gunman. Kleinhans put away the three guys in the paper this morning and that guy Servi they found in the park. Servi was paying him off, and they were in on a caper to get $120,000 from the mob. Have someone check his car, his house, and his bank account. You should find a machine gun and more money than a cop should have. Check his hand gun against the bullet in Servi."

"Got it," he said. "I'll tell the right people."

"See you around."

"Need anything?" said Daley.

"A new body and some blood," I said, fading away. "I hope you make it to the White House."

"I hope you make it back to California," he said. He hung up.

"I hope I make it to tomorrow," I said to myself.

"Finished?" asked the nurse.

"I hope not," I said, but I don't think my words came all the way out. I faded into something between delirium and sleep, and stayed there for forty-eight hours. My dreams were great. Koko the Clown and I had a snowball fight in Cincinnati and won millions of chips for drinks at Kitty Kelly's. Harpo and Koko danced. Chico and Al Capone had a nonsense debate, and Groucho ran for vice-president under Richard Daley. The snowball fight gave Merle G. a cold, and I had to visit her in the hospital.

I remember looking down at her and saying, "You really got yourself into one, didn't you?"

My eyes opened and I realized the voice wasn't mine. It was hers. I was the one in the hospital being looked at. She was the one talking.

"Hi," she said. "My cold's gone."

"Great," I said, my mouth cracked and dry. "How's my bullet hole?"

"Coming along," she said. "Doctor got the bullet out. He says you should be up and out in a day or two."

"Hey, that's great."

"Yeah," she said. "Everything's great. The cops don't want you anymore, and Nitti's not looking for you. That's what Ray says. He talked to the Marxes. They talked to the cops."

"Great."

"Great."

Silence. In the hall a woman cried and said, "Te amore, madre."

"You going back to L.A.?" Merle said.

"As soon as I can," I said.

"I brought your suitcase."

"I would have come to say goodbye," I said. "Say, can you give me some water?"

She did and I thought.

"How'd you like to come to L.A.," I said. 'I could probably get you a job, and we—"

Her head was saying no, but she was smiling gently.

"Can't go," she said.

"The kid?"

"Yeah," she said. "You never asked about her."

"None of my business," I said. "But I wanted to know."

She considered telling me, looked out of the window at the falling snow, bit her lower lip, shuddered and said,

"No, maybe next time."

"I'll be back," I said.

"Like hell you will," she said and leaned over to kiss me. "Life is like a movie to you. One day you'll get killed and won't get another role. You're no damn cartoon dog who comes back together after being cracked or flattened." I tried to hold her, but I had no muscle for the effort. She pulled away.

"You've got the address and phone number if you feel like reality," she said. "Take it easy."

"I can't," I said.

She shrugged again.

"O.K., then, be careful," and she was gone.

The room was just big enough for a bed, a metal closet, and a small window. I was alone, no ward. I sat up. It made me dizzy, but it didn't hurt as much as I expected. I was bandaged tight and wearing a hospital gown. When my foot hit the floor, a guy who looked like a real goddamn doctor came in. He was tall, grey, tired, and wearing a suit. A stethoscope hung around his neck.

"Peters," he said, pushing me back gently, "anyone ever tell you you were a medical wonder?"

"Yeah," I said. "A kid doctor in L.A. named Parry."

He listened to my heart, thumped my chest, took my blood pressure and talked.

"You have another gunshot wound no more than a

year old," he said. "Several wounds from sharp instruments, multiple scars and bruises, a skull that should be
picked for posterity, and a variety of broken bones
which have healed remarkably well. Your septum is
also badly deviated."

"And I have the worst lower back in Southern
California." I added.

"You're worthy of Grand Rounds, Peters," he said,
looking into my eyes for signs of further decay, "but we
have an even more interesting case. Nineteen year old
brought into emergency in a stupor, grand mal seizure
and vomiting. He was sweating and lethargic with slight
abdominal tenderness. Trouble breathing and respiratory infection. You're a detective. You know what
he had?"

"Homesickness?"

"No," said the doctor, "One hundred and eighty
little rubber bags filled with cocaine powder in his
stomach. He was sneaking them in from Columbia,
South America. Could have killed him."

"I'm enlightened," I said.

"You're all right," he said. "Bullet didn't hit anything, lodged in a muscle. You lost blood and you'll
have to change that dressing in a few days, but if you're
up to it, you can leave tomorrow."

"Thanks," I said. "By the way, I can't pay cash for
all this."

He stuffed his stethoscope in his pocket, being sure
that enough stuck out to identify him.

"All paid for," he said, "by your physician, Dr.
Hugo C. Hackenbush. I told him all about your case,
and he agreed that you could leave, but suggested that

you see him and his associates in Los Angeles."

"I will," I said. "Thanks, doc."

He left with his back straight. Ten minutes later a nurse came in and helped me walk around the room. She was a little thing with Barnum muscles.

In the morning, I got a long-distance call and a pair of short-distance calls. The long-distance call was from the Marx Brothers.

"In my medical opinion," said Groucho. "You're cured. And we've decided to help your career by not telling Louis B. Mayer what you've done for us."

"Thanks," I said.

"Your pleasure," he said.

One of the other two calls was from an accented voice. I thought at first it was Chico Marx, but I changed my mind fast.

"You got one day to get out of the city," the man said. "Twenty-four hours. You understand?"

I said I did and he hung up. I got out of bed and started walking around the room and through the halls. Then I got my second local call. It was from Ray Narducy. He wanted to know if I needed him or his cab.

"Tomorrow morning at nine be in front of Cook County Hospital."

"Right," he said, moving into a heavy British accent that might have been C. Aubrey Smith, Charles Laughton, or Cary Grant. "I'll be out there with bells on."

I spent the rest of the day walking and tallying my expenses in my black book. I listed the losses at the Fireside as "essential information paid for." The figures filled six pages. I couldn't read a few in the front because blood or ketchup had gotten to the pages.

My figures came to $867.14. I added forty bucks for my return trip to L.A. and twenty bucks for a suit to replace the one with the hole in it. Then I called Warren Hoff, collect. It was after six in Los Angeles, but he was in his office.

"Toby," he said sadly. "It's good to hear from you, but I've got bad news. Mr. Mayer says you're fired. I tried to reach you two days ago at the LaSalle, but you'd checked out. He says you didn't get results, and he won't pay for the last two days."

"Tell him I love him, too," I said, "and that Chico Marx's problem is taken care of."

"I think he'll have mixed feelings about that."

My eyes wandered to the blackness of a late February afternoon in Chicago, and my rear end itched. I wanted to be on a plane.

"Warren, I'm submitting a bill for $927.14, and I have to be paid fast.

"I'll do it," he said.

"I don't want you to pay for it," I said. "I want Mayer and MGM to pay for it."

"Mr. Mayer will pay for it," he said. "He pays for what he orders, even if he doesn't like it. I just don't think you'll be on his favorite people list."

"Well, I'm in good company," I said. "See you in the sun."

I didn't sleep much, just listened to the same woman in the hall moaning "madre mia" and "amore", the cars skidding in the night and ambulances screaming from unknown directions.

In the morning I put on my last remaining pants, a

wrinkled shirt, and my coat. I said goodbye to no one and tried to find the moaning woman, but couldn't. She could have been any one of three down the hall.

Narducy was waiting for me on a day almost as dark as the night. Rain was falling. Thunder was cracking, and the piles of filthy black snow were being eroded to make room for the next cycle.

"Supposed to go down to zero tonight," said Narducy, taking my suitcase and helping me into the front seat of the cab. He put my bag in the back seat.

"Streets'll be an ice pond from Summit to Evanston," he said, getting in and looking at me. "Geez, you look like Halloween."

I looked in his rear view mirror. I reminded me of a skeleton mask I had worn when I was a kid.

Narducy drove me to Midway airport and helped me in. He didn't do any imitations. He bought me a seat to L.A. with a stopover in Denver for fueling. I had seven bucks left after I paid Narducy. I bought him a sandwich while we waited and invited him to visit me in Los Angeles. I didn't know where I'd put him or what I'd do with him, but it seemed like the right thing to say. He said he'd think about it. He shoved his glasses back, downed an egg sandwich in three bites and his Coke in four gulps.

"Carramba," he said, wiping an imaginary mustache. "That was good."

His timing was bad. There were no Mexicans around.

There was a stand-up bar in a corner and I bought a glass of wine. I went back to the sandwich counter where I had left Narducy and paid extra for a glass of orange juice and a raw egg. That left me with three bucks.

I took the Fleming cold remedy over to Chaney who was sitting at a bench with Costello, watching us. They weren't trying to hide. I handed the drinks to Chaney, who was blowing his nose.

"On me," I said. "It's good for a cold."

"Thanks," he said and downed the drinks. "Doesn't taste bad."

I didn't say goodbye.

The plane took off just before noon. From the window, I watched Chaney, Costello and Narducy get smaller and disappear in seconds. The rain was still coming down. Just before we hit the clouds, I took a last look at Chicago. It looked green.

A stewardess with a blue uniform and blue cap brought me sandwiches and asked if everything was all right.

A chubby guy with a big mouth and a briefcase sat next to me at the window. He had a Southern accent and talked about how much flying he did. When we were about half an hour out, he turned pale and said the engines had stopped. I couldn't turn any more pale than I was. The engine hadn't stopped, but what was left of my heart did.

About six hours later, I got off the plane in Los Angeles. The sky was filled with smog and the sun was grey and warm.

With the few bucks I had left, I took a cab to my office and left a light tip. By the time I made it through the downstairs door into the lobby darkness of cool tile, the smell of Lysol, and of the bums, I was down to my last twenty cents.

I almost never used the building elevator, but I made an exception in this case. My side was stiff and sore and in need of a change of venue. I clanked upward, working out supplementary expenses in my mind in case Mayer asked for a detailed breakdown.

The office door was just as dingy and the pebble glass just as dirty as I had left them less than two weeks earlier. There was one difference. Just below "Sheldon Minck, D.D.S.," there was a thin crack that curved down through my own name. Someone had used four pieces of adhesive tape to keep it from getting worse. I opened the door gently and tiptoed through our minute waiting room piled high with old magazines, uncleaned ash trays, and forgotten junk mail.

Through the second door, I found Shelly Minck—short, myopic, cigar in mouth, and sitting in his worn dental chair reading a professional supply catalog.

He looked at me over the magazine.

"Where you been?" he asked casually. "You've been gone a couple of days. I was beginning to worry about you."

"I've been gone almost two weeks, Shelly," I said, searching for a semiclean cup so I could pour myself some of the rancid mud Shelly kept going as a service to favored patients.

"What happened to the door?" I said.

"That's a tale," he said, shaking his head and covering his upper lip with his lower. "Remember Mr. Stange?"

"Old guy with one tooth left you were trying to save?"

"That's the one," he said. "As soon as I finished the work and started to fit the bridge, he tried to hold me up. Used one of my own instruments—sharp little thing I've never known what to do with."

"O.K.," I said, finding a cup and rinsing it in the jet of water near his dental chair. "What happened?"

"I gave him six bucks," Shelly said, warming to the tale and removing his cigar so he could gesture. "Just as he went for the door, Jeremy Butler came in."

Butler was our landlord, a former pro wrestler who

now managed his property and wrote poetry.

"Well," continued Shelly, "I told Butler what was happening and be grabbed Stange. Stange stabbed him in the arm, but Butler paid no attention. Just lifted him up by the neck and took the weapon and the money from him. The window broke when he threw the old guy at the door. That's why I'm reading this book."

"O.K.," I said. "Why are you reading the catalog?"

"To find out what that goddamn instrument was for. So how was your trip?"

"Not as exciting as your week here," I said. "Just four bodies. And I got shot."

"Too bad," he said, without really hearing. His head was back in the catalog.

I went into my office. It was stale. I opened the window and sat in my chair, looking out over the low buildings. I felt better. I examined the cracks on the wall as I drank the coffee and looked at the picture of my brother, my dad, me, and our dog Kaiser Wilhelm. Then I looked at the pile of mail in front of me. There were seven or eight letters and a few messages scrawled by Shelly.

The most important piece of mail seemed to be the one at the top—an envelope from MGM complete with a little lion in the corner. There was no stamp, which meant it had been delivered by a messenger. I tore it open and found the check. I thought I could breathe easier with almost a thousand bucks. I tried it. The pain in my side told me to be careful breathing.

There was a message to call my brother. I called him.

"Lieutenant Pevsner," I said in my best smart-ass

tone, "to what do I owe the pleasure?"

"You owe the pleasure to a hearing on your license," he snapped.

"What the hell for?" I cried, causing myself further pain and dropping tar-thick coffee on my hand.

"For all that crap in Chicago," he said. "The Chicago police called for your records and listed you as wanted in connection with three murders."

"Four," I said. "That's all been cleared up. The Chicago cops cleared me."

"Maybe they're more forgiving than the license review board."

"Oh come on, Phil," I tried. "There is no license review board. Just an Irish lawyer in the mayor's office who does what you guys tell him."

"Maybe," he said in something approaching glee—a state he seldom achieved unless he had his hands on me. "You write up a report on the whole thing," he said. "I'll ask Donovan to review it if I'm convinced."

"You have a great heart, Phil."

"You've got a big mouth Toby. I heard you got shot. How are you?"

"A little itchy, but all right."

"Too bad," he said. "Goodbye."

"Hey," I said, catching him before he hung up. "How are Ruth and the kids?"

He called me a name and hung up. Asking him about his wife and kids always drove him halfway up the wall. I wasn't sure why. I always figured it was because I spent so little time with them, and I was his only brother. It got him raging mad, but it had also become a little ritual with us—something we both expected and couldn't stop. I considered calling him back and saying something. He was my only brother, and I had seen a lot of other people's brothers in the last week or so. I considered it, but I didn't really. There was nothing I could say to Phil. It was too late for us to do anything but for me to shoot wisecracks at him while he shot punches at me.

I finished the coffee and kept going through the mail which included:

— An invitation that looked as if it were printed on soiled paper. It was for a seance with a Swami at a dime store in Burbank. For two bits he would tell the future of everybody who got there on Thursday between three and five.

— A letter from a lady who wanted to know if I was any relation to a writer named Peters who did her favorite children's story when she was a kid. She had seen my name in the phone book while looking for a detective. I hoped she found one.

— An old hospital bill. From the date, I couldn't remember what I had been in for. I guessed it was for my back or concussion. My calendar didn't help me.

— An ad from a bank telling me they'd give me a pocket watch just like the old time railroad men wore if I deposited $500 or more in a savings account with them and promised not to take it out for a year. The ad had a picture of the railroad watch and a little chubby engineer holding it proudly.

— A message to call someone named Abe. I though I could make out the number and guessed that it was Abe Gittleson, the guy I had done some work for who owned a pawn shop. I decided to call him soon and make a deal for the coat I'd bought in Chicago.

— A letter I was afraid to open.

I had purposely put the letter on the side. The handwriting on it looked familiar. I stalled for another minute or so, wiping my hands, throwing envelopes in the trash basket that no one had cleaned while I was gone. Then I opened it. It was from my ex-wife Anne—Anne Peters, née Mitzenmacher.

The letter:

Dear Toby,

The last time I saw you you staggered into my place like a sick dog looking for whatever you could get. I told you to stay away. Now I'm asking you to give me some help.

Don't get your hopes up. This is not a plea for you to come back. It's a combination of two things. A request for help from and to an old friend, and the offer of a job I think you can handle.

The job is confidential and very important. The pay will be very good.

I tried to reach you by phone several times, but that dentist you share space with had no idea where you were.

I can tell you that it involves a man named Howard Hughes, and some things that are vital to the nation's security.

Please call.

Anne.